The Shadow Catcher

Also by Andrzej Szczypiorski
from Grove Press
The Beautiful Mrs. Seidenman
A Mass for Arras
Self-Portrait with Woman

The Shadow Catcher

Andrzej Szczypiorski

TRANSLATED FROM THE POLISH
BY BILL JOHNSTON

Grove Press

New York

Published simultaneously in Canada
Printed in the United States of America

FIRST PAPERBACK EDITION

Library of Congress Cataloging-in-Publication Data
Szczypiorski, Andrzej.
  [Złowić cień. English]
  The shadow catcher : a novel / Andrzej Szczypiorski : translated
from the Polish by Bill Johnston.
      p.   cm.
    ISBN 0-8021-3565-X (pbk.)
    I. Johnston, Bill. II. Title.
  PG7178.Z3Z3813   1997
  891.8'537—dc21   96-47370

DESIGN BY LAURA HAMMOND HOUGH

Grove Press
841 Broadway
New York, NY 10003

98 99 00 01   10 9 8 7 6 5 4 3 2 1

The Shadow Catcher

He was woken at six. Outside the window the sun was shining and the birds were singing. The early morning was warm; it was going to be a hot day.

When he opened his eyes, the thought that the long-awaited moment was here made him shut them again abruptly. He was afraid that after all it was just a dream. Then he leaped out of bed and pattered barefoot across the shining, waxed parquet floor. He washed quickly; suddenly every second had become precious. He looked in the mirror over the wash-stand and was surprised by his own pallor. Large hazel eyes, shaded by thick lashes, gazed out at him. He had a rather high forehead topped by a thick, dark shock of hair. When he was younger he had liked to tangle his ink-stained fingers in it.

In the bathroom a slender brick-colored water heater, encircled by a metal band, stood on the floor on two bear's-feet. The surface of the stove was smooth and cold. The boy pressed his cheek against it.

Then the family had breakfast together. His father ate in silence, occupied as usual with his slices of bread, which he spread carefully with butter, decorated with cold meat, chives, and sometimes even cress, and then consumed heartily, using a knife and fork, which was wont to induce an embarrassed admiration in the boy. His mother was, as always, on edge, with difficulty forcing herself to be patient and calm, atremble with an inner energy that she was never able to apply; she drank her tea reluctantly and pecked at crumbs of bread roll and jam, at which time her tongue, pink and narrow, would appear suddenly on her lips, filling the boy with dread.

Everything in the dining room glistened and seemed broken up by the light. He may have had this impression because they had never before eaten breakfast at such an early hour and he wasn't used to this avalanche of sunlight flooding through the window. The sun lay across the floor and the carpet, irradiating the cut glass on the dresser; and when he placed his hand on the tablecloth, he felt the unfamiliar warmth of its early rays.

At seven his father stood up from the table, wiped his lips on his napkin, lit a cigar and, holding it between his teeth, went up to the slim grandfather clock in the corner of the room. He opened the door and began to wind up the works. The chain creaked and the golden weights rose upward. Seven chimes rang out. The boy's father puffed on his cigar, and his head was wreathed in bluish smoke. At this point the boy's mother, as if moved by a desperate premonition, jumped up from her chair, stroked the boy's mop of hair, and ran from the dining room. He heard the tapping of her heels far away in the apartment, then her high, birdlike voice speaking to the maid and demanding her hat and her bottle of eau de cologne.

They left home at a quarter after seven. The sun was already hot. In front of the gateway to the building two horse-drawn cabs were waiting, because they had a lot of luggage. The asphalt of the roadway, heated by the previous day's sunshine and then cooled during the night, was dappled with the marks of hooves and automobile tires. There was a smell of tar, dry weather, and warmed stone.

The boy's parents took their seats in the first cab, while the boy sat in the second with the maid and the luggage. The concierge, a thickset old man, bid them farewell with a bow and a tip of the cap.

The horses' hooves clattered on the asphalt; the cabs moved along swiftly, since there was not much traffic. They crossed a bridge, under which flowed the river, yellowish, broad, and shallow because of the long hot spell. In the middle of the river there extended a sandbar connected to the riverside by a stone dike, on which the boy noticed the figures of anglers.

They reached the station on time and were able unhurriedly to find seats in a compartment of the train as it waited to depart. There was a smell of dust and leave-taking. The boy's mother declared:

"These carriages are filthy."

"I'd say rather that they're sad," responded his father. He sat down by the window and carefully lit a cigar. Suddenly, on the platform there appeared an elegant officer. His spurs rattled as he walked. He was looking into each compartment, his head tipped back. When he saw the boy's father he stopped and saluted. The boy's father lowered the window; his mother gave a delighted cry, leaned out the window, and gave the officer her hand to kiss. Behind the officer an orderly appeared, laden with suitcases. Later, that orderly stood in the corridor for the entire duration of the journey . . .

"Hello there, young sir," called the officer to the boy when he entered the compartment. Then he added to his parents: "How time flies. Krzyś has turned into a young man, he's changed beyond recognition. How old are you, Krzyś?"

"Fifteen," replied the boy. He didn't remember the officer. So many people passed through his parents' home.

"In a few years I'll have you in my regiment!" exclaimed the officer.

"Fortunately, he's not fitted for the army," said the boy's mother. "He's so frail."

"He's strong and healthy," said his father.

"What nonsense," said his mother.

The compartment was stuffy even though the windows were open. Nevertheless, they made themselves comfortable, the boy and his father by the window, his mother and the officer in the middle. The maid sat silently by the door, while outside the door the orderly stood and sweated.

At last the train moved off. Ugly suburban landscapes passed by the windows: shacks, allotments, soot-blackened houses, ramshackle huts. Carts harnessed to thin, shaggy ponies rolled along the dirt roads between the buildings, while dogs lazed in the shade of lilac and acacia bushes that were no longer in bloom. Then the city disappeared and the train sped across lowland meadows, flat as a tabletop, flooded with summer sunlight, devoid of shade.

The boy's father and the officer were speaking about the international situation. His father said:

"And yet I can't shake off a nagging sense of unease . . . "

"Trust me, doctor," replied the officer. "There really is no cause for concern. Hitler is encircled."

"I don't trust the French," said the boy's father. "They're so self-seeking."

"We have a treaty with England."

"True," said the boy's father. "We have a treaty with England."

Exhaustion sounded in his voice. The boy's mother was rubbing her temples with eau de cologne.

"I beg you, gentlemen, let's not talk of war," she said. "We've already lived through two; that should be sufficient for our generation."

All of a sudden, she looked anxiously and tenderly at the boy.

"Krzyś," she said, "you've gotten hot, darling."

"No, I haven't," answered the boy.

The officer irritated him. Perhaps because he had never, even in his earliest youth, wanted to be an officer. Such an existence seemed to him something incomplete. In his childhood games he had sometimes been a commander in chief, sometimes a rank-and-file soldier in the trenches, but never an officer, a character that he was quite simply unable to situate on the battlefield. For him an officer was a person without a role.

The train rumbled over a viaduct then once more ran across meadows. The boy was dreadfully thirsty. The grown-ups were talking. Again there was an argument about war—whether it was possible or completely out of the question. The boy dozed. He dreamed of a pond, a boat, him in the boat, completely alone, at dusk, in the moment after sunset. He dreamed that he was happy, but he knew it was only a dream. Because in his waking hours he never experienced complete happiness. Except maybe in the darkness, after the light had been turned off, just before he fell asleep, when his thoughts froze in total isolation from the outside world, when he felt truly on his own, alone on the whole planet. Then he would say to himself the following words, with profound conviction:

"I love you, God. I love you, Mama. I love you, Papa. I love you, Berta."

Berta had been a bitch who had died of old age not long ago, the companion of his childhood. Then he would add:

"I love you, Grandmother. I love you, Krzyś . . . "

And he felt slightly embarrassed that he loved himself. And it was just at that time that he experienced great happiness. Then he fell asleep. At peace, as never in the course of the day.

The train slowed; the dull thud of the ties could be heard, and at last the cars pulled up at a station platform. Cries rang out from the merchants selling candy, soda water, ice cream, and pretzels.

The boy was silent. He knew they wouldn't allow him to drink water from a station vendor. The boy's mother believed in microbes. He believed in nothing except God and love.

The adults' conversation died down; the oppressive heat gagged them. The compartment became quiet; the train continued on its way, and once again there was the regular clatter of the ties, and every so often the piercing whistle of the locomotive rang out . . .

Most of all he liked Sunday afternoons, which, for as long as he could remember, he had spent at his grandmother's. Sometimes he wondered, in a lazy sort of way, why he was so fond of those quiet, solitary after-dinner hours. He had no need of the presence of his grandmother. He even felt a certain delight when she retired to the other end of the dark, somewhat run-down apartment, where she immersed herself in handiwork that was partly amusing and partly touching. On white linen cloth she embroidered flowers and fantastic birds that shimmered with extraordinary colors.

At such times he would sit alone in the spacious dining room.

The apartment house in which his grandmother lived was old, damp, and gloomy. She occupied an apartment on the second floor of an outbuilding separated from the main building by a dark courtyard full of cooing pigeons. The street was in the center of the city but was quiet; pedestrians appeared there infrequently, and vehicles even less often.

The dining room, unlike in his parents' home, always seemed dark, cold, and thus immense. On the walls, hung with cherry-colored wallpaper, were paintings in heavy gilt frames. The canvases were blackened with age; he was unable to make out any of the pictures except one, which depicted a boat on a stormy sea. Beneath a cloudy, almost navy-blue sky surged rolling waves, on the crest of which rode the boat with swelling sails. He could discern the outlines of the people on board, but could not see their faces. This filled him with dread and a pious concentration of his thoughts. He had no wish to be one of those poor souls, at the mercy of the elements; and he was often touched to think of their unknown fate. Did they reach the shore, where their families anxiously awaited them? Or did they sink to the bottom, all trace of them lost?

The other pictures in the dining room didn't capture his attention so. Yet he liked to gaze at the painting of a lovely young lady with fair hair and rosy cheeks, in a crimson gown and a hat that threw her face into shadow. He knew that it was a girlhood portrait of an aunt of his by the name of Magdalena, a nice lady whom he was fond of, a plump and rather too talkative person who, when she visited his home, always showered him with kisses and candies. He was amused by the expression in his aunt's eyes in the portrait: childlike and at the same time rapt, an expression he had never observed in the eyes of that good, corpulent lady.

And yet if the truth be known, what he most liked to do was to sit without moving on a chair at the great oak table, rest his chin on his hands, and abandon himself to outlandish thoughts. He was always pleasantly surprised by this, enchanted even. For, throughout the whole week his mind had been taken up with various matters concerning school, his classmates, his games and pastimes; and now, suddenly, on Sunday afternoon, in his grandmother's dining room, he became a completely different boy. And yet he waited for these moments, which he regarded as his secret . . .

Oh, how delicious it was to be thinking at the great oak table! Everywhere there reigned a silence that rang in his ears, broken only from time to time by the clatter of horses' hooves from the street, the cooing of pigeons outside the window, or the abrupt chiming of the clock striking every quarter of an hour. Then he was alone. And that feeling of solitude seemed to him something beautiful and precious, though he also sensed a certain dread. He would look at the cherry-colored walls, the heavy, motionless pieces of furniture, which seemed to him like sleeping animals, at the inscrutable canvases in their gilt frames. He would pick up old postcards, a multitude of which lay on the dresser, and pore over the curious landscapes—unknown mountains and beaches, railway stations or hotels on green hillsides, where a carefully drawn arrow indicated the window of a room where the sender of the card had once stayed. He wondered what they had looked like, those people from the time when his grandmother still received messages from the outside world. Without difficulty he found pictures of them. Amongst the bric-a-brac that had accumulated in the drawers of the dresser he would come upon pasteboard photographs of slender ladies in huge hats decorated with feathers, and gentleman in the tight-fitting uniforms of armies that no longer existed. He also found photos of funny, rectangular-shaped automobiles, which he didn't think could run. Next to these odd machines he could see gentlemen in caps and great leather gauntlets that reached up to their elbows, mustachioed, standing stiffly upright or with one knee bent, resting a foot on the wide running board of the car.

He was extremely fond of those apparently vacant moments, when he communed with a distant, incomprehensible past, with an unknown world that existed without him and outside of him. At such times he experienced a certain sweet feeling, and he knew that it was precisely the thought of things passing that was so dear to him. At these moments—and only in the dining room, in the darkness and silence of an empty summer's day—he also thought about God. He thought he sensed His presence around him, though he was not certain of it. He was troubled by the thought of what had been even earlier, before the gentlemen in leggings and spats, before the ladies with slender silhouettes forever shading their faces with parasols to shield themselves from the sun. And what was even before that, on the other side of the dark surface of the pictures that no one could make out anymore. Then he was troubled by the thought of what would come afterward, in a hundred years, two hundred, two hundred thousand. Yet when he tried to penetrate that abyss of time, his head spun, he was beset with dread, and he would open his eyes and wish not to think any longer.

He was also extremely fond of everything that preceded those Sunday visits to his grandmother. It was quite possibly those mornings that most occupied his attention throughout the whole week.

On Sundays he slept longer than on ordinary days, but he could never understand his classmates, who found pleasure in lazing around in bed almost till noon. By nine o'clock he would be out and about, gazing at the sky. It always galled him that his Sunday, his plans for Sunday, were contingent on powerful forces no one could control. A clear sky he would greet with relief and thankfulness. Clouds irritated him, rain depressed him. He didn't like the rain, unlike many of his peers. He found no pleasure in wading up to his ankles in puddles or lifting his face to a downpour. A wet shirt sticking to his body he found a nuisance. He liked cleanliness, warmth, and a mild wind.

He was one of the many boys in the world who do not overly appreciate the charms of winter. He often thought of those southern lands, hot and sunlit, where dry winds fan the leaves of the palm trees. He heard the rustle of those leaves, which reminded him of the rattle of tin sheets.

He liked to walk barefoot over warm sand, which, unfortunately, he was able to do rather infrequently. He also liked it when sweat trickled down his back in a warm, narrow stream, and he liked that dryness in his throat. Winter always seemed to him something heavy, breathless, and stiff.

And so he was glad on a Sunday morning when the sky was cloudless and the sun shone softly. Then he would set off to visit his grandmother. The people on the streets were in their Sunday best and walked with a stateliness and calm that he never noticed on weekdays. The little girls had bows in their carefully braided hair. The boys showed off freshly ironed trousers and gleaming white shirts. On street corners, here and there horse-drawn cabs waited for passengers. He liked the smell of those cab ranks. It was a distant, unreal smell, the same one that enveloped him when he read tales of the adventures of medieval knights.

The horses snorted jauntily, and the harnesses jangled on their backs. The air was bitter and pungent with the smell of horse sweat, old leather, oats, and urine. Whenever he passed by a cab rank he would always think that it was high time to become an adult. Yet a moment later he would be running, skipping, or tunelessly whistling the opening of a military march. It was always the same march, because there was only one melody he could remember and had grown to like. It was the triumphal march from *Aida,* which he had heard once on a gramophone record; but he had decided that it was his march, the song of his army as it marched into victorious combat. Because, of course, he had his own army, of which he was the commander in chief. Yet quite often he dismissed it to the barracks of oblivion, where it led a quiet existence and from time to time reemerged in his imagination, each time in a different uniform, under new regulations, and with new generals, whose names he thought up somewhat hurriedly, almost at the last moment before battle.

And so he set off to meet his grandmother. She would be waiting for him on a bench near the entrance to the park. She always had on the same clothes, or at least so it seemed to him. In the summer she would wear long, dark dresses gray or crimson in color and made of a fine material that she would say was called georgette. As he drew near, his grandmother would smile at him and call:

"How are you, my little rascal!"

"How are you, Grandmother," he would reply and kiss her on the cheek.

Her cheek was soft and flaccid; with his lips he felt a soft down, and this always amazed him. His grandmother smelled nice, different from his mother and his aunts, different from himself. There was something indescribably delicate and light in that smell, and at the same time a distance, something alien and almost repulsive. It was the smell of leaves in early fall or of the bark of trees after rain, and also of mushrooms when they have been partially dried.

His grandmother often used to say that he had her eyes.

"You have my eyes, you rascal," she would say.

And so he would almost always look into her eyes in order to read himself in them. He liked his grandmother's eyes. They were large, with a greenish iris and a very dark pupil, in which there was always a spark of gaiety.

To begin with he would sit on the bench next to his grandmother, and for some time they would be silent. On the sidewalk in front of them the Sunday crowds flowed gently past. Adults came by on their walks, somewhat puffed up like turkeys or peacocks, and with them their children, running and jumping about, clamorous as sparrows.

He was very fond of his grandmother. Perhaps partly because, unlike all other grown-ups, she never inquired about how he was doing in school, about his grades or his classmates. Once he asked her why she didn't try to find out about these things. She stroked his cheek with her limp hand and said:

"Because that's your life, you rascal, not mine. If you want, you'll tell me of your own accord."

He decided that his grandmother was very wise. Another time he said:

"I can tell you about school, but I think it might be boring . . . "

"I think so," answered his grandmother. "It's not of interest to an old woman."

"And what *is* interesting?" he asked.

She laughed quietly. For a moment she was silent. Finally she said:

"The other side."

He looked at the opposite sidewalk, but quickly realized that his grandmother had been referring to something else.

He touched her hand. A strange emptiness filled his mind.

"Which other side?" he asked, and his throat felt dry.

"Death," his grandmother replied calmly. "You know that death exists."

"I do," he said quietly.

"Don't think about it," said his grandmother. "You have time enough yet. Lots of time . . . "

She fell silent, kissed him on the head with immense tenderness, and added:

"But less than you might imagine. It all goes by so quickly!"

"Grandmother," he said urgently, "I don't want you to die."

"I don't want to either, you little rascal," she answered, and laughed almost joyfully.

Then, as always on a fine Sunday, they went down the steep, deserted lane that ran alongside the park railings to the small square where there were ponies for hire.

He had his favorite pony, which he most enjoyed riding. It was a rather ancient creature, chestnut-colored, with a sentimental expression and a lazy imagination.

When he had been small and did not yet attend school, for his Sunday rides his grandmother would hire a little carriage lined lavishly with straw, to which the ponies were harnessed. But when he grew older he rode on the pony's back. A few years ago it had been only a make-believe pleasure, for Mr. Edzio, the owner of the ponies, would lead the animal by the bridle, and the boy had nothing to do but to stay in the saddle. Mr. Edzio was a talker. He always told the same stories about his ponies, which, in his opinion, were extraordinarily clever; they understood human speech and from time to time were even able to say something interesting to their master. Yet this never happened in the presence of other people, but only in the stables outside the city, and usually after sundown.

At first he believed it all; later he came to realize that Mr. Edzio was nothing more than a friendly trickster who was trying to amuse his young clients. After some time Mr. Edzio stopped telling his stories.

"You're a big lad now," he once said. "You find my tales boring."

The boy heard a note of melancholy and disappointment in Mr. Edzio's voice. Edzio was tall and lean; he smoked cheap cigarettes and had stiff, dark hair that stuck to his skull. He liked his own stories about his ponies and was sorry to lose listeners just because they were growing older. For this reason, he most liked to give rides to little boys who weren't yet of school age. Yet he respected his established clients, with whom he was linked by a certain familiarity.

And so usually they would go down the steep lane to the square, where Mr. Edzio would welcome them and rent them a pony for an hour.

The lazy chestnut mare was called Eliza. She greeted the boy with a certain dignified joy, tossing her head, while her soft, mobile nostrils sniffed about for sugar cubes.

When he was seated in the saddle she would move off at a walk up the steep lane, and when she had climbed all the way to the top she would turn around gaily and set off back down to the little square at a gentle trot. And in this way, to and fro, first uphill slowly then trotting back down, they would ride for an hour. During this time the boy's grandmother would sit on a bench in the shade of a parasol. Sometimes she would eat cherries from a large paper bag; sometimes she would read the newspaper. Each time he rode past her, she would look up and call:

"You're captain of the uhlans, you rascal!"

He wasn't pleased at this. At the time he was being a general, an Olympic champion horseman, or even the famed Sitting Bull, undefeated Indian chief. But most often he was simply himself. And when he turned fourteen he grew bored with Eliza, the steep lane, Mr. Edzio, and his grandmother's cherries. He was increasingly reluctant to walk down past the park railings, but he didn't say so straight out, because he knew it would hurt his grandmother. He was aware that this old woman was less able than he to tolerate change.

After some time his grandmother realized that he had grown older. He noticed that she had become sad. Now they went on walks in a different direction, along the broad avenue in the park. At the end was a pond; on the pond there lived swans, which people fed with bread and cheese. Next to the pond was a café; they would sit on the terrace at a marble-topped table, on uncomfortable garden chairs, and his grandmother would take tea while he had ice cream or fruit and cream. The afternoon hours passed them by in silence and sweltering heat. These were times when his grandmother thought ever more intensely about death, and he about life. They were becoming unnecessary to each other, but they were bound by the past.

It sometimes happened that the boy, driven by compassion and love, asked his grandmother if they could go down the steep lane to the ponies like before. She seemed surprised and pleased by this. She looked at him out of the corner of her eye, and the spark of gaiety in her pupils burned more brightly. Mr. Edzio greeted them effusively, and even Eliza pricked up her ears.

The boy patted the pony on her matted coat; they talked with Mr. Edzio for a while, then they returned slowly up the hill. These were bitter moments for both of them. They no longer felt what they used to feel before.

One Sunday, as they were coming back up the steep lane, the boy's grandmother said suddenly:

"Going back never works, my dear . . . "

By that time she no longer called him "my little rascal," but "my dear," which he preferred.

That Sunday was the last time they went down to the square with the ponies. He never saw Eliza again.

In this way, then, for many years he had spent Sundays with his grandmother, first playing in the sand in her care, then riding ponies, and finally in the park café at the marble-topped table. Invariably, through all those years, around two in the afternoon they would go to his grandmother's home, that gloomy apartment building on the quiet downtown backstreet. And invariably, through all those years, as far back as he could remember, the two of them ate dinner together in that dark dining room, surrounded by the pictures in their gilt frames.

The dinners his grandmother made had an incomparable taste. He especially liked the desserts, which were extremely fancy, consisting of fruit, cookies, creams, ice cream, and chocolate.

Grandmother had a serving lady, a very old and uncommunicative woman whom the boy always found unfriendly. For this reason he avoided his grandmother's kitchen, entering it only when he had to.

After dinner he usually remained alone in the dining room. His grandmother would disappear into her bedroom, where she was awaited by colored threads and pieces of linen stretched in frames. Her serving woman clattered the dishes at the other end of the apartment; he could hear the sound of running water, the distant hiss of the gas flames on the stove, and sometimes his grandmother's cough as she bent over her embroidery.

And that was how the afternoon hours passed, silent, warm, yellowish—from the partly closed shades—which made the boy think of the time after dinner on Sundays as being like a piece of amber warmed by the sun and lying on a sandy beach, somewhere at the very ends of the earth.

And like a fly in amber, the whole past in that room was ancient and unmoving.

In spring, summer, and early fall his Sundays ended long after sundown. It may have been just this experience that made him dislike winter so much. For in winter, nighttime was quite simply absent from his life! His day in the winter consisted of dark early mornings, when the sky looked as though it had been thickened with cream; short daylight hours, which even in sunny weather seemed somehow opaque, as if they were covered by spiders' webs; and finally long, endless moments of evening twilight, which was not actually night. Everywhere there was movement and noise: In the dark tunnels of the streets there were the bells of trams and the clop of horses' hooves, from the open doors of stores and restaurants the light from chandeliers spilled out onto the sidewalk, mixed with billows of steam— in a word, the day went on, somehow artificial, and for this reason jarring, an unnatural day that refused to give up its place to the night . . .

Whereas the late evenings of summer and fall allowed the boy to find out about nature as it slept. When he was on his way home from his grandmother's, walking through the almost deserted streets, in the mild, tender glow of a setting sun, his ear caught the cries of birds falling asleep in the treetops. The sparrows gradually fell silent and the black wings of swallows appeared ever less frequently against the pale patch of sky between the apartment houses. Here and there a dove would coo, awakened by the noise. The day was going out like the fire beneath a kitchen range, and it was only occasionally that a breath of wind rekindled the dying sun in the west, again reminding the boy of the last bright little flames of a fire. The roofs of the buildings, usually gray or almost black, now gleamed like gold or copper. The last rays of the sun slipped across them toward the sidewalks and roadways, and lingered upon the bark of trees, windowpanes, and the leather harnesses of horses.

Then everything was extinguished and the night exuded darkness. The streets fell silent; somewhere a church bell rang eleven times; the moon and stars appeared over the rooftops of the apartment buildings.

Sometimes he would count the stars, gazing at the sky, standing still on a street corner, head tipped back, face somber, intent with the effort, consumed by the excitement of that fearful calculation. He counted and counted till his eyes watered, his neck was cricked with pain, and his heart was filled with a sweet and cruel secret, from which he fled in his thoughts toward everyday matters of the following day's physics or geography lesson.

He liked hot and breezy nights, when the wind blew down the streets, lifting the dust from the roadway and the sidewalks, making curtains billow out from windows like sails.

And it was only at these times that he liked to look at girls, who were always older than him, since those of his own age would no longer be out on the streets. He himself had that privilege because when he had reached the age of thirteen, his father had declared that he was a fully mature boy and had lifted any conditions regarding when he had to be home, how he should dress or comb his hair, what dishes he should eat, or how he should acquire knowledge. Besides, his parents were so busy with each other . . .

And so he looked at girls. Once—it was in the fall, at a quarter after nine in the evening, when he was on his way back from his grandmother's, along a busy downtown street lit up by the neon signs of theaters, bars, and nightclubs—he stopped by a display cabinet with movie stills. The pictures showed Indian braves, white outlaws, and beautiful singers from a saloon in the Wild West. He stared at the photos while crowds of pedestrians streamed past behind his back. All about there was a smell of coffee, nuts, and carpenter's glue, because right by the theater there was a café and a furniture shop. A tram was squealing along the tracks, and from a lighted gateway came loud music and the tipsy voices of the patrons of a dance hall. From the open windows of the mezzanine, where there were billiard halls, could be heard the distinct crack of cues against balls, the short, sharp sound of bells that indicated a hit, and the muffled voices of several men.

It was right at this moment—in that setting of the big city immersed in an acrid fall evening—that for the first time he experienced such a painful feeling.

Someone tapped him on the shoulder, and when he looked up without thinking, he met the eyes of a girl. She had thick ash-blond hair, full lips, and an intense expression on her face. She was wearing an organdy dress that was too light for the time of year, and she looked as though she was quite simply dying of cold. And yet he noticed that her forehead was damp, and was amazed that someone could simultaneously be hot and cold.

She said quickly, in a somehow angry voice in which he heard a keen note of dread:

"Give me your arm. I'm your sister."

"I don't have a sister," he responded, but he gave her his arm.

The girl pulled him into the crowd on the street. They walked along quickly and unevenly. He felt the warmth of her hand, heard her shallow breath, and when he looked to the side saw her profile, indescribably beautiful, greenish in the neon lights, like a sculpture or a death mask. He was wracked by a shudder of disquiet and a manliness he had never before known. He was prepared to stand up to the entire world, if only it would make this girl breathe more easily.

Suddenly he noticed that they were the same height, and that he was even a tiny bit taller than her. Suddenly he felt that her hand was less firm, frailer, weaker than his. Suddenly he realized that his step was longer, and that she had to hurry to keep up with him. He slowed down a little. Then she said:

"Come on. Quickly, quickly!"

He moved in front slightly. Now he was leading her by the arm instead of her leading him.

"How old are you, kid?" she asked.

"Fifteen," he lied, for he was fourteen and four months.

"You're a grown-up young man," she said. Again he noticed perspiration on her forehead and a damp line under her nose and beneath her lower lip.

"Why are you running away, ma'am?" he asked.

"I'm not," she retorted. "I'm not running away."

He sensed tension in her voice. All of a sudden she stopped; they looked at each other. Her unease was gradually ebbing away. They entered a dark gateway. Here cold rose from the old stone floor. There was a smell of horse urine and freshly laundered linen. There was a pressing shop in the courtyard.

"Thank you," said the girl.

"Who was after you, ma'am?" he insisted, in a rather harsher tone, astonished by his own boldness.

"You wouldn't understand. You're fifteen . . . "

"And you?"

"What's that got to do with it? Next month I'll be twenty. I'm too old for you."

And suddenly she put her arms around him. He felt her breasts under the organdy dress and experienced a feeling of rage. Rage such as he had never before felt in his heart. It was almost animal-like. He felt like biting this girl, tearing at her breasts, her neck, her arms, her face.

He rushed from the gateway like a madman, took to his feet, and kept running till he was completely out of breath.

And then, when he stopped on the sparsely peopled square shaded by ancient trees, in silence and darkness, he thought to himself that he had not yet experienced love.

Because that had not been love, what had happened to him years ago, when he was seven, in first grade, and he and his father had gone on a boat ride up the river . . .

He was delighted at this adventure. His imagination crossed the threshold of his experiences hitherto and, like the river boat, sailed out into open water. This had probably been the intention of his father, who was bringing up his child wisely. He was an intelligent and educated man who was aware that it was impossible to develop his young son's inner life without ever-new stimuli and the constant development of his understanding of reality. Yet his father must have been amazed to see how quickly the boy grew in the space of those few days of life on board.

The boat was small and narrow, painted with white oil paint. It was driven in the old-fashioned manner by two paddle wheels that ceaselessly churned the water. They sailed along slowly, amid the lowland landscapes; along each bank extended the river bottoms and meadows flat as tabletops where cows could be seen. Here and there a tree was indicated by a black mark against the sky, while a fisherman dozed in its shadow, crouching on a rock. The skein of dark smoke from the smokestack stretched out behind the boat as far as the eye could see.

The weather was pleasant, and so the company spent most of the time on deck, where they lay on deck chairs from morning till late evening. Since this was one of the more expensive cruises, the passengers mostly belonged to the class of people who are well-off and have become somewhat idle, with a fond-ness for cards, liquor, and rather easy mores.

The boy in no way felt the lack of others of his own age on the boat. In fact, he spent virtually the entire trip in the distant, mysterious, imagined world of his adventures. Naturally he was the captain of the boat, and he was traveling up the Mississippi to buy precious furs from the Indians of the interior, paying for them with guns, beads, and horse harnesses.

The captain stood for days on end in the prow of the boat, searching for signs of Indian life on the horizon. Sometimes the smoke from a village appeared; then, rounding a turn in the river, he would spot wigwams, herds of grazing cattle, and braves prancing on their horses. Then he would give the order to moor at the riverbank.

When the deckhands had carried out his order, the merry company would disembark and travel in horse-drawn cabs to the nearby town, where there was usually a historic Baroque church or a famous inn. Nevertheless, and despite his father's attempts to persuade him, he would remain on board to con-duct his complicated trade with the Indians. He would purchase furs and sell muskets. He had to keep a close eye on his drunken band of sailors, and also foil the Indian warriors, who were out to cheat him. Usually he was able to manage with the use of his fists, though on a few occasions he had had to reach for his gun. Once it happened that he shot an Indian who had thrown a knife at him. He jumped nimbly out of the way; the knife lodged in the boards of the deck and quivered for a long time. At this moment he shot from the hip. The Indian staggered and col-lapsed at his feet.

It was quite a complex scene, for he had to be both himself and his opponent. First he would throw the knife as the enraged Indian, then he would jump aside nimbly, fire from the hip, run to the other side of the narrow deck, and drop dead on the wet planks.

Just at the moment he was picking himself up in order for the Indian to turn into the captain of the boat once again, he met the amused gaze of a young lady who was leaning on the railing of the upper deck and observing him.

"Who are you?" she asked.

He was a polite and well-mannered boy, and so he clicked his heels and bowed. He told her his name and who his papa was. The lady was disappointed.

"No, I wasn't asking about that," she said. "Who are you now? A buccaneer?"

He was embarrassed. He shook his head. She walked slowly down the steps and came up to him.

"I thought you were a buccaneer," she said. "You just killed the officer who was guarding the black slaves. . . . Will you set them free?"

"There aren't any slaves here," he said in a slightly more confident voice. "I'm the captain of a boat on the Mississippi and I moored at the riverbank to buy furs from the Indians. They were trying to cheat me . . . "

The lady grew a little worried; she bit her lip and looked about watchfully.

"They could be very dangerous," she said. "They don't like the white traders. So many times they've been double-crossed."

Suddenly she gave a cry and bent over.

"Watch out!" she called. "They're shooting at us! They have poisoned arrows—"

He wasn't exactly thrilled at all of this. Now it was his turn to bite his lip. He was wondering how to let her know that he really didn't need her and that her ideas about poisoned arrows were quite simply stupid. She had spoiled his game; she wanted to take part in it, but there was no room for anyone else in his closed, colorful world, where the strong prairie wind ruffled the manes of galloping horses, there was the whistle of musket balls, the ropes of the old boat creaked, the song of the sailors rang out as they drank their gin, and barrels of gunpowder rumbled as they were rolled across the deck.

She had appeared out of nowhere in the crowd of unshaven deckhands and half-naked Indian warriors in her green summer dress and green pumps, a bracelet jangling on her wrist, and had changed everything round, messed up the story that he had pieced together with such care and that was developing so wonderfully, where chance could of course thwart his plans, but only if the Indian who had been hit by the bullet with his last remaining strength had, for instance, pulled a pistol from his belt, or instead of falling on the deck had tumbled into the waters of the river. But it would never have been possible to reconcile his imagination harmoniously with that of another person; in fact, that may have been precisely the reason why he preferred to play alone even when he was among his classmates. He disliked the arguments about which of them would be the Indian and which the white man, who would be in command of the platoon retreating from the trenches outside Verdun, and who would pilot the reconnaissance plane that was landing at the order of the general staff.

. . . That was exactly why he lived his own life and didn't let his peers into his world.

But those peers had at least some idea of what was going on. None of them would have had the crazy notion of firing poisoned arrows at the deck of a merchant ship by the banks of the Mississippi at the very moment when important business transactions were taking place. It would have been like taking the story of General Nobile's ill-fated expedition to the North Pole after his dirigible crashed and mixing it with the story of some brawl in Texas or Arizona.

"I guess you don't feel like playing with me," said the lady.

He nodded and felt deeply sorry for her. Once again she had hurt him. Maybe from her perspective it was playing. For him it was as real as anything. She was the one who looked somewhat unreal, in her halo of thick hair, with green shadows on her eyelids, willowy, slim, and ethereal as the mares he sometimes used to ride on his ranch in Colorado, where he grazed his horses. She was quite unlike all the women who occasionally made an appearance in his life—dressed in thick skirts, colorless, faceless—and who constituted at best a background to events somewhere in a besieged blockhouse or on an army bivouac, in the ruins of a fortress, where they would sneak through at dusk, bringing food to the men or moaning with fear at the thought of the enemy attack that was to take place at dawn. Those women were virtually incorporeal, whereas this lady seemed to him to be nothing but body, devoid of all meaning. She was composed of hair, face, neck, arms, hips, legs, eyes, hands; but she lacked a concrete existence, she had no role to play, and her attempts to prove herself a useful participant in events were truly pathetic . . .

He stood somewhat helplessly on the deck, uncertain of how to act in order to delicately remove this woman from his life. Chance came to his rescue, for a tall, slim man appeared on the gangway, laden with bags full of fruit. He had come back from the local town, where he had bought supplies for the next stage of the journey.

When the lady saw him she instantly lost interest in Indians, poisoned arrows, and the fur trade.

The boy was once again alone on the deck and was able to drive back the attack by the drunken warriors, who, ignoring the musket fire, were attempting to storm the immobilized boat. But the battle had already died in his imagination. He looked around and saw the sun-drenched deck of a small river boat, a blackened smokestack, light sprinkled upon the windows of the small dining room, and a little farther off the empty backwaters, a horse grazing in the high grass, and a roughly paved road, along which a dust-covered chaise was traveling.

He was alone, utterly alone, and even his bold crew, so inured to the hardships of sailing the dangerous waters of the Mississippi, had disappeared somewhere. He saw the lady in the green dress talking on the upper deck with the athletic-looking man, and he felt a sharp pain in his heart. He became aware that he was a little boy, and that his world was a world of make-believe, which fell apart at one carelessly uttered word.

He went back to his cabin. Bright sunlight streamed in through the round porthole, while from outside came the plashing of water. He lay down on his bunk, closed his eyes, and wanted to sail off somewhere else. Since the reflection of the sun off the surface of the river was dancing on the white ceil-

ing, he turned his imagination to the South Seas. He was strong
enough to transform himself in a single moment from a trader
in the Midwest into a sailor who had lost his way on the ocean
as he traveled to the islands of Fiji. Fortunately, it was a clear
day and there was no danger of a hurricane. He was able to steer
his little ship easily, straining his eyes in search of land.

But something was wrong on this journey. Now he was no
longer alone on deck, and he didn't feel like a solitary castaway;
he was oppressed by the presence of another person. When he
carefully scrutinized the deck, everywhere, in every moment and
every situation, he could see at his side the woman in the green
dress, who was staring at him with a hint of friendly irony. He
decided that she was a passenger who had been saved from the
wreck of a transatlantic liner and whom he had found on a desert
island; and he reconciled himself to this. But in such a way he
accepted her presence; he was forced to put up with her company, and even to think about her in moments of peril. He took
responsibility for her life and her safety, which restricted his
freedom of action. Two people on the deck of a lost boat: That
was a different story entirely! It occurred to him that he would
have to share his meager food rations with this woman, and at
once he changed the state of his supplies, increasing them con-
siderably. After all, he hadn't gone to sea in order to mortify
himself!

When a storm drew close, he was mindful of the woman;
he told her to take shelter belowdecks, while he himself, in
indescribable torrential rain, in an onslaught of thunderclaps
and towering waves, ably operated the sails. But even in the most
dramatic moments, when he should have been concentrating

all his attention on the wet, slippery ropes that were sliding out of his grasp, he could see the terrified face of the woman cowering in the cabin. To begin with he shouted:

"Don't be afraid, ma'am, I can manage!"

Yet he quickly abandoned his good manners. When she appeared before him again, shaking with fright, he cried sharply:

"Don't be afraid, woman! Bail out the water!"

He threw her a bucket, and she obediently began to scoop up the water, which was already ankle-deep. For some time he watched the woman's movements as she bent over, filled the bucket to the brim, straightened up, and then leaned her whole body out to tip the water overboard. Every one of those movements of hers, so harmonious and flowing, caused him pleasure.

Suddenly he heard an ominous creak from the masts and came to. Once again he was alone on deck and was struggling with the rigging.

It was exhausting. And all at once he had had enough of the South Seas, the hurricane, and the sense of danger. He looked around his cozy cabin; he got up from his bunk and went back on deck.

Three-quarters of an hour later they set sail. Once more, lowland meadows and herds of cows passed by on each bank of the river, and on the horizon there were villages, above which rose slender columns of smoke.

A gong rang out resoundingly, and the whole company sat down to tea in the dining room. The boy's father had brought chocolate, fruit, and the latest newspapers from the town; immediately after his meal he buried his nose in the papers. At this moment the lady in the green dress passed by their table.

"Did you defeat the Indians?" she asked with a smile.

"No," he replied. "But I rescued you from a desert island."

Everyone around laughed. Everyone except the lady herself. She gazed intently at the boy and said:

"I must have been terribly helpless and afraid."

He nodded.

"You couldn't count on me," she added.

He nodded again.

"How strange," said the lady, turning to the athletic-looking man. "He's such a small boy, and yet he knows me so well."

The man gave a laugh. He had beautiful teeth, like a movie actor. But the woman was still serious.

And it was at this point the boy thought to himself that maybe he was unhappy. He developed a dislike for the tall, elegant man who, he had decided, was the cause of all the woman's cares. And at the same time he felt a strange sense of solidarity, of absolute reconciliation and understanding, which deserved a sacrifice. It didn't last long, maybe only a moment, or maybe for the entire duration of the river trip. . . . But it remained in his memory as a precious experience, of a sort that he never knew in his contacts with his peers, neither before nor in later years. And he returned to that experience, which intensified as he grew up, until one fall day, at dawn, when he woke up abruptly, and it drew forth from his throat a groan of fearful longing for that woman without a name, now without a face even, her features obliterated by time, voiceless, lacking even those details that once accompanied her, the color of her dress and her hair, the expression in her eyes, the shape of her hands.

. . . There remained in him only the memory of her existence, which demanded compassion, care, and, above all, closeness.

And that was why he suffered, because he realized he would never again see that woman, who may not even have noticed his presence in her life.

By the time he reached the age of fifteen, he already knew it had not been love. But he also knew that it was then, on the deck of the river boat, all those years ago, that for the first time he had known a longing for love, a longing that never left him again.

It was at this time, when he turned fifteen, that he took up a curious occupation which usually draws older people but is found among the young too: He decided to review his life thus far. Oh, he didn't think about it so seriously; it was just that for the first time he began to wonder whether there might be something wrong with him. To put it even more plainly, he stopped liking himself and began to notice scratches and disagreeable cracks in his image.

He looked about himself and realized that he was completely alone.

If the truth be told, he had never liked school. Every morning he would go there with a certain reluctance. It was easiest in the winter, because at that time nothing in the world existed that could attract his attention. But in the spring and the fall he was loath to give up the morning hours. He always had the feeling that school was stealing his freedom. He envied his fellow students who came to class contented and even seemed to some extent to have missed the clamor of the school, the desks carved with penknives, the black rectangle of the chalkboard. He wanted to be one of them, but he never achieved that carefree easiness of thought, that lazy irresponsibility, which he observed in his peers.

School had been a torment to him from the very first day of lessons.

He clearly remembered that day. They had dressed him smartly; he smelled of the brilliantine they had put in his hair to make it lie flat. He had been given a brand-new suit; and precisely because it was so new, he felt terrible in it. On his back he carried an empty satchel, which seemed pointless to him. It was a warm, sunny day. His mother led him by the hand.

"Don't be afraid, sweetheart," she said as they crossed the park on the way to the school.

He wasn't in the least afraid. He was curious rather.

The schoolhouse seemed to him immense, dismal, dark. It had been built long ago; at the entrance two giants hewn out of stone kept watch. The corridors smelled fresh and foreign; it was hard to keep one's balance on the polished floors.

All of a sudden his mother disappeared, and he found himself beside a large, stout woman in eyeglasses. This woman became his first teacher; from her he learned how to make letters into words, and words into sentences. She also led him into the jungle of numbers and helped him to recognize the shapes of landmasses on the map.

She was a kind, indulgent person; yet when he lost contact with her after two years, the features of her face, the sound of her voice, and her gestures were quickly effaced from his memory. All the same, he retained a certain affection for this first teacher of his life, and when afterward he ran into her some-times around the school, he always felt good for a moment.

The classmates he met that day were suntanned seven-year-old boys in short pants and white shirts. He could never under-stand why they were so restless, so talkative and obstreperous.

It was at this time that he had his first contact with others of his own age, and he was profoundly disappointed. During the breaks they would race like madmen down the long corridors, make a fearful racket, fight, pull one another's hair, or kick a ball frantically around the crowded, dusty playground.

He kept his distance from them. During the lessons he stared out the window, watching the clouds drifting by over the rooftops. At these times he would think a great deal about the trees in the nearby park, about squirrels, dogs, and cats. He also thought about birds, which he adored. In the classroom he felt the absence of wind, leaves, clouds, the clatter of horses' hooves on the cobblestones, the squeaking of the tram, and the river that flowed through the center of the city, over which two black-and-ginger-colored bridges basked in the fall sunshine like ante-diluvian lizards.

In the classroom he never lost a sense of confinement, of captivity. He yearned for open spaces, and the lack of them made him feel threatened.

And yet he didn't find it difficult to learn. He was a good student; he wrote neatly and clearly, and did his sums quickly and accurately. But he didn't enjoy these successes. He was oppressed by a solitude that he was unable to come to terms with. At school he felt alien, different from everyone else; it was only years later that he understood that almost every one of his class-mates had similar concerns.

Just how wrong he had been to think himself different, alone and isolated, he discovered only at the age of fifteen, when he asked his peers the names of their own classmates from first and second grade. How few they remembered!

To begin with they would give one name, a second, and a third. Then a worried note sounded in their voices. They searched their memories in intense concentration, more and more alarmed that they were finding nothing. One more name, and then another; but these were already separated from the person they belonged to, barren, meaningless.

They would shrug somewhat dispiritedly. This question had led some of them to put the workings of their memory to the test for the first time, and they had experienced a bitter letdown.

Everything that had constituted their school life in the first years of their education had turned out to be impermanent and transitory, as if they had dreamed of some event, then had woken up and could recall only fragments of it, from which it was impossible to build a coherent whole.

At this moment he felt a sense of relief, for he now knew that he was not an exception, an oddball, a curio, a cripple . . .

But his isolation in the school was not complete, for he had his teachers too. Two of them became a part of his life: One with an awkward charm, rather embarrassedly, in a stream of words and eccentricities from his exuberant personality; the other abruptly and stiffly like a corporal in the barracks.

The first taught Polish; he was known both in school and

out as an accomplished poet, and his name could be seen in booksellers' windows and in the newspapers. His appearance brought to mind readings from the literature of the last century. He was a huge man with strong shoulders, a large head going somewhat bald, and the luxuriant beard of a prophet, which flowed like a ruddy torrent onto his broad chest. In his youth he must have been uncommonly handsome, and with his students he was wont to recall his past, full of minor scandals, amorous adventures, caprices, and foolishness.

He was in the habit of treating the students as friends; he attempted to reduce the sense of distance, and he often took on the pose of a good pal. He was demanding yet tolerant. He liked to help the weaker students, but while he was about it he never lost an opportunity to make fun of them a little in front of the whole class. He sometimes used coarse words, and also employed school jargon: Words like *cheesy*, *ragging*, or *jeepers* were forever on his lips. He also had his own sayings, which the students adored. When someone was called to the front and gave an unsatisfactory answer to a question, he would send him back to his desk, uttering the time-honored sentence:

"You can kiss a dog on its nose, but watch out that it doesn't turn around, or you'll be in a pretty pickle . . . "

The class would greet this aphorism with a burst of laughter, and the teacher would stroke his ruddy beard solemnly and flash a roguish glance from behind his eyeglasses.

The other teacher who stuck in the boy's memory was a slim man with exceptionally refined manners. He wore a cassock, which, in contrast to most priests, set off his slender, almost feminine figure. He had splendid gray hair and a dry, well-proportioned profile that was rather Roman and also ascetic.

He wore a gold-framed pince-nez. He carried himself upright; he always amazed people by his cleanliness and his attention to every detail of his priestly attire, which was somehow difficult to reconcile with his monkish, rather absent gaze, his quiet voice, and the nervous gestures of his hands. In his right hand he always carried a long, thin pencil, with which he would mercilessly rap the ears of students who made a mistake when called on to answer in class.

The Polish teacher was someone whom the students were able to deceive without difficulty. The catechist inspired respect mixed with fear. Yet that giant with the ruddy beard succeeded in spite of everything in implanting in the hearts of those boys a love of literature, whereas the priest did not awaken in them the fear of God. In his lessons, God became, as it were, the result of mathematical equations, or was not present at all. They learned a great deal about His attributes, but He Himself remained foreign and distant for them. When it came down to it, in the religion classes there was more literature, while in the literature classes there was more divinity, perhaps because of the Polish teacher's magnificent beard and his indulgent kindness.

The boy suffered because religion became a dead subject for him. He felt within himself a thirst for mystical experiences, though he wasn't able to express this.

One day he summoned up the courage for a one-on-one talk with the catechist.

On that day religion was the last lesson, and after his classmates had left the room he remained alone with the teacher. Outside the window a late-fall rain was coming down. The early November dusk was slowly setting in.

"What do you want?" asked the catechist. His pince-nez gave off uneasy flashes.

"Is God good?" asked the boy very quietly.

"God is good," replied the priest.

"And all-powerful?"

"And all-powerful," replied the priest.

"So He can prevent people from suffering?"

"He can do anything. But through suffering God puts people to the test."

"So that they'll attain salvation?"

"So that they'll attain salvation," replied the priest.

He stood in his black cassock against the black chalkboard, and the gathering twilight blurred the outlines of his figure, only his gray hair standing out clearly. With the tips of his fingers he held the long, thin pencil, which trembled in the air as if it had been infected by the man's inner tension. The priest's voice was icy, almost offensive; his words cut through the silence like a knife cutting the pages of a book.

"I have a headache," said the boy, and then added quickly: "What about animals?"

"What do you mean when you ask about animals?"

"Can animals attain salvation?"

"No," answered the priest. "They don't have souls."

"Then why do they suffer? God has no need to put them to the test, because they can't be saved."

"God does that which He sees fit. It is not our business to ponder His judgments. Do you have a headache?"

"A bit of one," replied the boy. "But I don't understand—"

"It is not our business to understand God's whims," said the priest and suddenly moved. His slender shadow detached itself from the chalkboard and passed in front of the bright wall. The priest stretched out a hand and turned the switch; the garish brightness of the lights flooded the entire classroom. The wind was lashing the rain against the windowpanes. The boy looked into the priest's eyes but could see only the light reflected in the glass of the pince-nez. He wanted to tell this man that his knowledge of God was of little value, and his love of God pathetic; but he lacked the courage and the ability to express this idea.

The conversation was over. He remembered it for a long time: So long that when there came a time of piety in his life, he sometimes prayed to God to forgive the catechist his faint-heartedness.

Whereas he never prayed for the bearded Polish teacher. He was utterly convinced that whatever else might be the case, the ruddy-haired giant had truly earned salvation.

He was fully aware, then, that his isolation in school would have been even more keenly felt without his contacts with these two teachers. "Redbeard," as the Polish teacher was known, had enabled him to some extent to come to understand and appreciate the value of solitude, thanks to his instilling a love of literature. He had pushed him toward the most disinterested form of love a person can ever experience: the love of books.

As for the priest, whose charming nickname was "The Lily," which in the later years of school changed to the more expressive "Torquemada," the boy owed him even more! For that teacher's stiff, petty, narrow-minded nature had forced him to take upon himself the onerous, sometimes even desperate task of independently searching for God.

Thus, only these two men had enriched his life and given

it new meaning. Apart from them and without them, school might as well not have existed for the boy.

They had arrived. Through the window of the compartment they saw a run-down little train stop. The filtered light of the dusk revealed the outlines of buildings in the nearby town. Birds were soaring over the rooftops of the low houses. Apart from the hiss of the locomotive and the voices of the few travelers who had continued this far, everywhere silence reigned.

As they left the train they noticed on the horizon, beyond the town, a dark line of woods to the east, where night was already slowly falling.

The company had already been traveling for almost a whole day in the hot, stuffy compartment, and so everyone was tired and out of sorts; a curious sort of tension, caused by numbness and lack of movement, had gathered in the recesses of their thoughts and feelings.

The boy's mother's slim heels tapped across the cracked concrete of the platform, which came to a sudden end and turned into a path that had become dried up with the heat. His father tipped his summery straw hat back on his head. He lumbered along, big and strong, carrying a rug over his shoulder, and also one of the suitcases, which he had taken from the maid to lighten her burden.

At this station there were no porters, but there quickly appeared two ragamuffins from the town, who for a few groszy were prepared to serve the gentlefolk from the capital. But they were beaten to it by a team of drivers sent from Nałęcz.

Nałęcz was their final destination. A village spread along the shore of a lake, or rather between two immense lakes, amid almost impenetrable woods that had not yet been discovered by civilization. In this Nałęcz there was a somewhat run-down manor house, the remains of a once rich and flourishing estate of the landed gentry. The manor house belonged to a friend of the boy's parents; and it was here that they were to spend their vacation.

In front of the station, then, there waited three wagonettes drawn by well-fed horses. The drivers bustled about smartly; the luggage was stowed in the last wagonette and the whole company moved off again. Long shadows of trees lay across the road, rutted by the farmers' carts. A mild, cool wind blew, and at last it was possible to breathe.

A problem arose as they were taking their places in the wagonettes: The boy's mother felt tired and longed for the chance to doze to the rhythm of a trotting horse and the soporific creak of the wheels. So in the end the boy took a seat in the second wagonette, along with the maid and the orderly. He sat next to the maid while the soldier, a ruddy-faced, resolute young fellow in an ill-fitting uniform, took the foldaway bench. He seemed to be extremely pleased by this turn of events.

They rode in silence. The driver urged the horse on with long moist clicks of the tongue; at these sounds the horse pricked up its ears and broke into a gentle trot. But a moment later it slowed to a walk, its head bowed to the ground as if it were looking for familiar ruts, only to speed up a moment later, spurred on by a click from the driver, its tail sweeping its hindquarters.

Night fell, still sultry and hot. A fine film of mist rose over the meadows; the birds ceased their singing, and stars appeared in the sky. The road began to climb slightly, and so the horses moved slowly, the harnesses tightened, and the wheels of the carriages squeaked monotonously.

The boy could hear the voices of his father and the officer conversing quietly in the first wagonette. Yet he couldn't hear their actual words, and he suddenly had the feeling that everything around him was unreal. The shadow of the driver on the box swayed regularly over the horse's rump; somewhere far off the cry of an animal he didn't recognize rang out and then broke off, plaintive and melancholy, and to the boy's astonishment, it came to him that soon it would be time for him to die . . .

When I die, he thought to himself, I'll see it all as it really is, in the light of day, while I myself will remain invisible. I'll see everything in the tiniest detail, every nook and cranny, every blade of grass, every droplet . . . I'll soar above the earth like a bird, and there will be no shadow anywhere. Everything will be clear, full, lush. Everything will be simple and understandable.

Once again he heard the strange cry of the animal, and a shudder of compassion ran through him.

"What's that?" he asked the soldier quietly.

"A stig," said the soldier.

"A stag, not a stig," said the maid, and burst out laughing.

"Right," said the soldier and coughed as if embarrassed.

The boy thought to himself that he knew little about the world. It was the first time he had heard the sound of a stag. He had been taken aback by it. He had expected it to be gentler, softer, and more melodious.

They drove into a forest. Here it was even closer; a motionless heat hung amid the trees, and it was only high up, among the leaves, that the rustle of the wind could be heard. They were plunged into darkness; even the shadow of the driver melted without trace into the night.

The soldier coughed again, and the maid laughed softly.

"We'll be there in a moment," said the driver as they emerged from the forest road. It grew brighter, for the moon was out and the stars were shining. The boy looked out from the wagonette. Somewhere, still far away, a light was flickering. The horse in its harness gave a sudden neigh and broke into a trot without being urged by the driver. The carriage swayed across the uneven ground.

At last they saw Nałęcz. They heard the barking of dogs, then human voices.

The village stretched in a circle along the shore of the lake, which at this time was shimmering silver in the moonlight. Further on there extended rushes, meadows, a sparse copse of trees; and then the shore of the second lake could be made out through the gloom.

At the edge of the village there could be seen the old park, damp and dark, and set back in it the manor house of Nałęcz, which had once belonged to aristocrats and today was virtually in ruins. It was there that they pulled up, driving in a semicircle around the remains of a lawn now overgrown with rampant weeds.

On the veranda stood a tall, gray-haired, round-shouldered man in breeches, riding boots, and a cloth jacket that bore the traces of military insignia that had been removed. Over his head he held a kerosene lamp, which cast the faintest of light on the crumbling, broken veranda.

Half an hour later, after effusive greetings, assignments to guest rooms, and the washing of hands in huge, cold basins, they sat down to supper in the dining room.

The boy had a sense of numbness; everything around him seemed plunged in an impenetrable haze, as if he were looking through a thick glass into an aquarium.

The dining room was large; it contained a rectangular table, high-backed chairs, and a dresser. Two kerosene lamps illuminated the interior. Over the door that led from the dining room to a playroom hung a set of stag's antlers, and next to them a picture depicting Golgotha. There was nothing else in the room.

They sat at the huge table, in the wan light of the kerosene lamps, from which soot leaked out in a thin stream. At supper there assembled a collection of odd and unfamiliar people, whose faces the boy was seeing for the first time. Along with his mother and father and the officer who had accompanied them on the journey, there was also the man of the house, whose name was Pilecki; his two elderly aunts in long black dresses, with lace shawls across their shoulders; a pale, diminutive girl with a timid expression; and finally a gentleman of around forty who seemed strangely embarrassed by the rest of the company. The boy knew he was the steward of the estate.

To begin with, fruit soup was served in a great white tureen, then veal with potatoes and peas, and finally raspberries and whipped cream, along with crumb cake. The gentlemen drank a homemade liqueur, which the host poured out with a certain unction. With every sip the steward closed his eyes in indescribable delight and said quietly:

"Exquisite. Truly exquisite . . . "

One of the old ladies, who was on the plump side, with a mild expression and a penetrating gaze, reminded the boy of his grandmother. It made him glad to watch her. She was spruce and well-groomed; her hair was tied neatly in a bun, while she had a network of wrinkles under her eyes and frail, almost transparent hands on which the veins appeared like cracks in an old sculpture. At one point the old lady said to the boy:

"I don't expect you remember me at all, Krzyś."

"I don't," he replied and smiled, a little embarrassed that he had hurt her.

"When I saw you last you were maybe five years old," said the old lady. "You were a pudgy little thing."

"He was only four then," put in the boy's mother, who had overheard the conversation. "It's true, he was ever such a little fatty."

"I remember that," said the boy.

He recalled a photograph he had had in his hand not long ago, showing a fat child in a warm little winter overcoat with a fur hat on his tiny head, standing in front of a garden fence. That was him, years ago. . . . Every time he looked at that photograph he seemed unutterably alien to himself. He didn't like that awkward, warmly dressed child with his vacant, stupefied, and somewhat timorous gaze.

Of course it was me, he thought, but not entirely. I think I used to like to run in those days, but how can you run if you're such a lump, such a bundle? I don't remember anything from those times. It's as if I'd been born a second time not long ago, as a boy who was already strong, tall, slim, and independent.

He sometimes looked at the hands of the child in the photograph. One hand was in a warm glove; the other was bare, and it was this one that drew the boy's attention. It looked like a shapeless wad or a badly baked roll, almost spherical, fingerless, devoid of strength.

Then he looked at his own hands and felt a sense of satisfaction. They were tanned, large, with long, slender fingers and well-shaped nails. When his hand tightened into a fist, he felt his own strength.

Supper went on; the dishes, from which the meat had disappeared, were taken away, and the raspberries and cream were brought in. The old ladies in their lace shawls were silent, prodding at their plates with their spoons. The tiredness that came with night rendered their features sharper; they looked now like anxious crows. The pale girl at the end of the table licked her lips with her tongue; a line of cream remained under her nose, but she didn't notice it and she became motionless over her plate, her elbows by her sides, sitting straight, silent the whole time, as if she didn't know human language, staring ahead somewhat mindlessly, somewhat in desperation.

The boy looked at his mother and thought to himself that she was beautiful.

So what if she's beautiful, he said to himself, if she doesn't love me. Oh, that's not true! Of course she loves me, very much even, but she's busy with a thousand other matters besides that love. Never, since time immemorial, has she had a whole, complete hour for me. Whenever I felt the need of her presence, she would receive me warmly, I admit, but with a kind of anxiety, as though she were worried that I'd rob her of some of the precious minutes of her own life. Constantly, from dawn till late at night, my mother has to be experiencing something new and exciting. I don't think she has even a moment to stand and think; there's something in her that won't allow her for the least second to stop moving, to look around and reflect. . . . Of course she loves me. No one loves me as much as she does! But it's *her* love, not mine. She has that love; I don't. She enjoys that love, while I can only suppose, can only hope that I'm loved . . .

He looked into his mother's face and bitterness filled his heart. She had never come halfway to meet him! His tribulations, fears, and doubts were never able to break through the thick shell of activity and perpetual motion that encased this woman's whole life. Whenever their conversations extended beyond a quarter of an hour, his mother would say in a pained voice:

"Don't pester me, sweetheart . . . "

And she was gone.

The boy thought with resentment and a little compassion that she had run away from his troubles not from an excess of her own, but simply because any troubles were disagreeable to her. When he felt lonely or was tormented by doubt, his mother would invariably run to the little chest of drawers in her bedroom, where among her fragrant underwear, light as gossamer, there was a small tin full of money. More and more often he thought to himself that she was defenseless and that she deceived herself into believing that she could buy security with ever-increasing expenditures. It wasn't just his troubles that she tried to relegate to the margins of her life, feverishly thrusting money into his hand for the movie theater, candy, or day trips. He had the impression that she made use of money the whole time, somewhat unthinkingly and impetuously, to free herself from incessant threats. Observing her, he came to the conviction that this woman lived in constant dread. One day he said so.

It was a late afternoon in early spring. She was just on her way out to town, wearing one of her beautiful, expensive dresses, fabulously colorful, accentuating her almost girlish figure, a hat with a broad brim, and long, cream-colored elbow-length gloves.

He met her in the hallway, where a faint light entered through the partly open door. He asked to talk with her, for he felt the need of his mother's company, though he wasn't able to say why.

His mother seemed, as usual, disconcerted and alarmed by his request.

"What do you want to talk about with me, sweetheart?"

"Oh, Mama," he murmured.

"I'm going out, you know. I'm already late—"

"Don't go," he said. "Stay with me."

She sat down all of a sudden on a wicker chair and rummaged in her handbag for a cigarette.

"What's wrong?" she asked and gazed watchfully into his eyes. She always looked like that when she wanted to express interest in him. At such times in her eyes there was dread combined with resoluteness, a sense of power mixed with embarrassment.

"Nothing's wrong," he answered. "Oh, Mama! You could talk to me for once."

"But of course, sweetheart. Something at school, I expect!"

She was always under the illusion that school constituted his entire world. Beyond school he simply did not exist. She seemed not to comprehend the fact that he too, quite independently of mathematics, biology, or Latin, thought, felt, and interacted with himself and with the world.

"At school everything's fine," he replied, sensing that he was being enveloped in the chill of indifference. On that wicker chair, a cigarette in her full red lips, in her close-fitting dress, she didn't seem to him to be as beautiful as usual.

She stood up abruptly and stubbed out the barely started cigarette with a rapid gesture, crushing it into the bowl of the ashtray.

"What is it then, sweetheart?"

"Mama," he said, "I'm alone."

"Alone?" she repeated with indescribable astonishment. "What do you mean, alone? You have Papa, me, our home, your friends! You have everything, sweetheart—"

"I'm alone," he said and felt a lump in his throat.

She was silent for a moment. She bit her lip. Slowly she removed the glove from her left hand. She pulled at the tips of the fingers of the glove and slid it off, baring her slender, beautiful wrist.

"Alone," she said quietly, as if this discovery had drained her strength. With her bare hand she stroked her son's hair, forehead, and cheeks.

"Before long you'll be grown up," she said. "My goodness! I only just had you, and soon you'll be grown up."

She spoke as if she had suffered a painful loss.

She looked into the boy's eyes.

"How handsome you are, sweetheart," she said softly. "Like Papa—"

"Don't say 'Papa,'" said the boy. "I don't like that."

"Why not?"

"I don't know. But I don't like it. Say 'Father.'"

She shrugged, and at once smiled in a conciliatory way.

"You're just like your father. He wasn't much older than you when I met him."

"I know," said the boy. "Father was your teacher. You were terribly bad at math."

She gave an easy laugh; in the dark hallway he saw her strong white teeth.

"Whereas your father was good at everything," she said.

At that moment, at the other end of the apartment the strident chimes of the clock rang out.

The boy's mother cast a startled glance at her left wrist, and began hurriedly pulling on her glove.

"Goodness, I'm terribly late!" she exclaimed.

"Do you have to go?" he asked quietly, almost humbly.

"Come along, sweetheart. Don't be dramatic."

She moved off toward the door. He stood in her way. She looked at him with unbounded amazement.

"What's wrong, Krzysztof?" she exclaimed.

She must have been deeply upset, since she used his name.

"You're always in a hurry," said the boy, his voice trembling slightly. "You never, ever have time for me. I can't talk to you. All you're able to do is ask if everything's all right at school. At school everything's fine, but what of it, Mama!"

"Come along now," she interrupted. "What do you mean, what of it? School's the most important thing. You have no idea how proud Papa and I are of every success of yours in school."

"Don't talk so much, Mama!" he cried.

"You're being quite silly, sweetheart! First you want to talk, now you don't! So what's the matter?"

He was silent for a time. In the end, he said with deliberation: "I don't know. I can't say."

"There you are. You see yourself, sweetheart."

How she irritated him at that moment. Every word of hers, every gesture hurt him, exasperated him. And suddenly, barely in control of himself, he seized his mother's arm above the elbow and said sharply:

"Mama, what is it you're so afraid of?"

At first she tried to free her arm, but when she grasped the meaning of his words she froze. For a second he could see tension and surprise in her eyes. It was as if he had uncovered something that was her deepest secret. But after a moment she said freely:

"How absurd! I'm not afraid of anything. And what exactly is going on with you? Let me go. You're just badly brought up."

He released her and stood back half a pace. She stared at him intently, as if she were recognizing someone else.

"Really, sweetheart!" she said. "I'm shocked."

She left rapidly, leaving the front door open. He closed it and went back to his room. He lay on the bed. He looked at the ceiling. He told himself that he didn't love her anymore. But he knew he did. He felt an indescribable sadness and disenchantment.

From that day on, when he thought about her, he thought: My poor mama! And she for several days avoided his gaze.

Now, in that huge dining room, busy talking with Pilecki, smiling and animated, though a shadow of tiredness showed as a dark line under her eyebrows—she looked captivating. In the pale light of the kerosene lamps, against the gloom that was gathering along the walls of the room, she seemed to the boy the most beautiful woman in the world. He thought to himself that she was egotistical, frivolous, beautiful, and beloved. And he smiled at her. And she, catching his look across the table, blew him a kiss; then she turned back to her easy, indifferent conversation with Pilecki.

Supper went on forever. The two old dears began chattering to each other quietly in their squeaky little voices. It was clear they were speaking about something cheerful, for the boy suddenly saw one of them laugh. She parted her old lady's lips, in this way making herself resemble a dead carp, especially as she had no teeth. The boy could see the strangely twisted cavity of her mouth, and around it the network of wrinkles that had suddenly sprung to life and were twitching on the skin that stretched the entire surface of her face into a grimace that looked more like pain than merriment. A terrible gurgling noise issued from her throat; that was her laugh.

The boy glanced to the side. He met the gaze of the pale girl at the head of the table. With his eyes he indicated to her the two old ladies enjoying themselves. The girl's own eyes moved slowly; the light was reflected in her pupils, which were oddly dilated, like a cat's in the darkness. The girl stared at the elderly ladies for a while, then turned and looked at the boy.

Over the crumpled white tablecloth two pairs of smiling eyes met.

The boy stood up abruptly, picked up his chair, and, unfazed by the reproachful gaze of his mother—who, as usual, attracted by movement about herself, was watching him—walked a few paces along the table in order to sit closer to the girl. She seemed a little disconcerted; once again she became demure, her elbows by her sides, stiff and absent.

"Good evening," he said. "We've not been introduced."

"That's right," she replied, still staring ahead.

"I'm Krzysztof. And you?"

"Monika," she said.

"Do you live here?"

She nodded.

"All year round?"

She nodded again. He looked askance at her, surprised that someone could live year-round in such a remote, godforsaken place.

"In the manor?" .

"Yes. With my uncle, Captain Pilecki."

Now he recalled some fragments of conversations from a month ago, when the coming vacation had been debated at home. Pilecki was an old acquaintance of his father's from the war. Together they had lived through many adventures at the front, which his father talked about only reluctantly, with a certain irritation even, whenever circumstances forced him to revisit those times. It was this that caused a cooling of relations between the former comrades in arms, for Pilecki lived almost exclusively through the memory of the war; he seized every opportunity to return to the stories of twenty years before, which angered the boy's father more than could have been expected or understood. Yet he also felt affection for Pilecki, an affection that was perhaps a little perverse and rooted in pride, for when all was said and done, during all those years that separated them from the trenches, the marches, the gunfire and stinking wounds, the boy's father had been laboriously moving upward, and eventually had acquired a position, a beautiful wife, costly furniture, trips abroad, suits of English wool, and French silk ties; while Pilecki had languished in the depths of Poland, in the back of beyond, tramping through marshes with a shotgun over his arm, out of boredom hewing oaken walking sticks tipped with shoemaker's calks—and just like those calks, he had slowly gone to rust. So the boy's father's affection for his friend from the trenches had a hint of lordliness about it; in Pilecki's presence, his father must have especially reveled in his unquestionable successes, for they had both entered the postwar world in the same sweat-soaked uniforms, with their packs on their backs and hope in their hearts, and while one of them had gone far, the other had remained in the rear of events, like a despondent straggler. Who knows if during the war Pilecki hadn't been ahead of the boy's father, which would have had an even greater impact on their present relations, which were friendly, yet not free of things left unsaid.

So back in Warsaw, a month ago, when they had been talking about their vacation on Pilecki's residuary estate, the boy's father had mentioned their host's niece, who was being brought up at Nałęcz. Years ago Pilecki had lost his brother and sister-in-law; he himself was unmarried, and he took the girl in.

So this is her, thought the boy, and looked at his neighbor with different eyes. He didn't find her particularly good-looking or alluring. She looked a little uncared-for, though her hair was tidy, her dress was respectable, and her hands were well-groomed.

I think she must be extremely unhappy, he said to himself, because she has no mother or father. . . . What nonsense! I have a mother and father, and it doesn't make me happy in the slightest. I find her uncared-for because I've been taught that orphans ought to be uncared-for, otherwise they're not proper orphans. While she looks better than many girls I've come across. True, she's skinny. . . . Her shoulder blades stick out; her shoulders are narrow, and she has a slight stoop. Maybe all the girls look like that in the country? Does she study? Will she become a housewife; will they marry her off to a farmer?

"Do you go to school?" he asked.

"Yes," she replied. "In a year I'll be doing my minor diploma."

"How old are you?"

"I recently turned fifteen."

"Me too."

"You're just a kid," she said.

"Don't talk nonsense, my dear."

He used that expression because he decided it was the most appropriate. "My dear" sounded protective, supercilious, yet at the same time good-natured. His father sometimes spoke to his mother that way. It irritated her.

The girl looked at him, smiled, and said:

"You're funny. I may grow to like you."

He felt embarrassed.

"You think I'm just a youngster," he said, planning a trap.

"Uh-huh."

"While you yourself are grown up?"

"Uh-huh."

"In this hole? What kind of a life can you have in Nałęcz!"

"The same as anywhere," she said.

"I live all year round in Warsaw."

"I know. So what?"

"The big city, that's all. The capital."

"And this is the country," she said. "I like it here."

He was silent for a moment.

"Don't worry," said Monika. "I like you already."

He shrugged. She was annoying him. Suddenly, for the first time in his life, he had accepted a style imposed upon him. So I'm not able to live in my own way after all, he thought to himself. What do I care if she thinks I'm just a kid? In reality I'm not a kid at all. Sometimes I'd even like to be, but I can't any longer. She's just stupid. A stupid country girl from the sticks.

"I told you, I like you," she repeated.

"So?"

"Nothing. It doesn't matter."

"Right," he said rudely.

"I'm glad you came. You'll make me laugh."

"I don't know how to make people laugh."

"Yes you do. You're doing it now."

I won't win with her, he thought. Not now, at any rate. Maybe even not ever. What's wrong with that? Do I always have to win? Have I ever won? I don't ever remember winning. It doesn't matter to me. She is the way she is. I ought to be the way I am.

"I'll try and keep you amused," he said.

Now she was embarrassed. He'd gotten away from her. She said coldly:

"You're not so much of a kid as I thought."

"I am, I swear to God!"

At this point the two old ladies rose from the table. One of them croaked that she was tired, that it was getting on to midnight and that she had to go to bed.

This was a sign that supper was over. The boy's mother and the gentlemen stood up from the table. Everyone's chairs scraped, and they all wished each other good night. The old man in the high boots came in, and behind him a barefoot village boy. They were carrying kerosene lamps. They stood them on the dresser, and Pilecki set about lighting the wicks. Yellow circles of light quivered on the ceiling. There was a strong smell of soot.

The host handed his guests the lighted lamps so that they could see their way to their rooms. The old ladies in their shawls, nodding their heads to each side, toddled off toward the door. Their shadows on the opposite wall reached up to the ceiling, where they bent across a thick black line.

"Good night," the boy said to Monika. "We'll talk tomorrow."

"Good night," she replied and smiled.

"Good night, sweetheart," the boy's mother said.

"Good night, Krzyś," said his father.

Everyone said the same two words, nodding their heads and moving to the door. Then they climbed the stairs to the second floor, where their bedrooms were situated. The stairs creaked. The boy's mother said something quietly to his father; his father laughed and put his arm around her. They mounted the stairs like two good spirits, in a tight embrace, while above them the light from the kerosene lamps slid along the wall.

"Good night, my friend," said Pilecki to the boy, when they reached the landing of the second floor. He continued with a heavy step further upward, to the attic.

Somewhere at the end of the long hallway the gleam of a lamp flashed and was extinguished by the closing of a door. It was one of the old ladies disappearing into her room.

When he blew out the lamp, he felt as though he'd gone blind. He was seized by fear. He lay in bed, feeling under him the stiff, starched sheet, indescribably cold and alien, smelling of straw, lake water, leaves, nettles, and wood chips burning beneath the hood of the stove. When he moved, he almost drowned in the soft rustle of the sagging mattress. He touched the rough wall with his hand, then ran his fingertips over the cold metal bedframe. He felt rounded, globular objects at the head of the bed: one, two, and three. He guessed they were bedknobs.

An impenetrable darkness surrounded him on all sides. He shut his eyelids tight, then a moment later opened his eyes wide, but still he could see nothing. He got out of bed uncertainly, felt for the floorboards with his feet, stretched his arms in front of him, and took two steps toward where he remembered the window being. He still couldn't see anything. His fear intensified. The thought that he had lost his sight added a sense of panic.

Here was the windowsill, and above it the cold, smooth surface of the pane. He felt for the latch, lifted it, and pushed the glass. The window opened quietly; he felt a breath of humid air on his face. Somewhere in the treetops the wind was at play.

Now at last he could see. Darker shapes of boughs and branches, and in the sky a solitary star.

Very slowly the darkness receded. He could already make out the outlines of trees in the park, and even the stone wall around the lawn amid the exuberant weeds. Far off, where there extended an endless pit of blackness, he spotted a delicate twinkling. It was the waters of the lake.

Once again he closed his eyelids and then opened them wide. His eyes watered from the effort.

He made out the shore of the lake, and beyond that its ruffled surface, which he sensed more with his hearing than his sight.

Then, suddenly he could see everything. He was amazed to find it wasn't so dark after all. He saw the park, the lawn, the lake, and even the shadow of a boat on the sandy shore. Not far from the veranda he saw the broken statue of a faun or goddess on a moss-covered plinth. He saw clearly the silhouette of the farm buildings, the steep roof of the barn, the broad wooden gates, and even the staple, barred at an angle. He could see the whole courtyard, and on it here and there brighter patches of trampled straw, ruts made by the wagonettes, and the tracks of horses' hooves.

And also the reflection of the star in the lake, between the trees.

And he thought to himself that for the first time in his life he was discovering the world with such intensity, with such attention and such a sense of security. Nothing could happen! That star would always shine over the lake, among the trees. And the wind would always comb the grasses, raising their bitter, warm green scent in a gentle dance. Nothing would happen!

He went back to bed; once again the mattress rustled beneath the sheet. He lay still for a moment, then with his hand touched the wall, the metal spheres on the headboard, and the surface of the sheet. He passed his hand over his own face, very thoroughly and carefully. First, with his fingertips he touched his forehead, then his cheeks, nose, and lips. Then his hand moved to his neck, his shoulders and his chest. Then it returned to the wall. His body was smooth, the wall rough; his lips warm, the metal bedknobs cold. But everything together seemed to him to be a unity; he was a small part of this room, the darkness, the night outside the open window. He was within the boundless world and felt himself to be an important part of the whole, and the entire world was within him and constituted what he was.

Thank You, Lord, for creating all this, he said wordlessly. And thank You for creating me . . .

Never before had he communed with his own life so keenly and so palpably. He felt he was alive. He heard the beating of his heart, his steady breathing, the pulsing of his blood. He had the impression that everything was alive along with him, or rather that he himself, thanks to an excess of himself, was conferring parts of his life onto his surroundings. The warmth of his body became the warmth of the blanket, and when he held his hand for a long time on the round form of the bedknob, its cold slowly dissipated, because he was heating it with himself, taking from it a little of its smoothness and lifelessness.

In the silence, suddenly he heard a whisper. He froze. The whisper reached him through the wall. He strained to hear it, but he couldn't make out the words. Yet he recognized that it was his mother's voice. In fact, she may have been speaking aloud. But all at once she became present, not down there, at the other end of the hallway, but by his side, within arm's reach.

Then he caught his father's whisper. And the ringing of a glass. That was his mother's happy laughter. Every time he heard her laugh, it sounded to him as if sunlight were ringing on crystal.

So they too were in this world that he was now absorbing, taking in his arms, to make it his own and at the same time to immerse himself in it as in the dark, yellowish waters of the lake.

Slowly he emerged from this bedazzlement onto the miry shore of sleep.

He awoke when the sun entered the room. He jumped out of bed and opened the window wide. The trees, the waters of the lake, the clouds in the sky, the barn, the gray statue of the faun with the broken-off nose, the nettles on the lawn, the straw trampled underfoot—and he himself, a slim, dark, good-looking boy with broad, muscular shoulders, long legs, a strong back, and slender hands.

He looked out the window at the expansive courtyard, unkempt and for that very reason attractive. He saw a short, thickset individual in riding boots and a green jacket, with a cap perched on his head.

This individual came out of the dark entrance hall; chickens ran about under his feet. He tipped back his head, looked at the sky, and sniffed. He passed his gaze along the windows, noticed the boy, and smiled in greeting.

"How did you sleep, young sir?" he called.

"Wonderfully!" the boy shouted back. "I think I'll go for a swim in the lake."

"The water's cold," said the steward. "I never go bathing there."

He went off in the direction of the barn.

At this moment in the courtyard there appeared a tall, thin Jew in a gaberdine and yarmulke. He emerged from the mass of greenery straight onto the path that led to the veranda. When the steward saw him, he stopped and turned back.

"Well then, Pinkus?" he asked.

"Well what? Nice day, just right for you, steward."

"Brought the horse?"

"What do mean, have I brought it? I was supposed to bring it, so I brought it," retorted the Jew.

"I'll take a look," said the steward, and headed off toward the acacia bushes.

"Is it an acorn?" asked the Jew.

"What?"

"Is it an acorn, that you'd find it up a tree?"

"Cut it out," said the steward. "So where is this little gelding?"

"Where's it supposed to be? Outside the gate. Is the master asleep?"

"The master went to Zagaje. Before sunrise. Boars have been rooting over there."

The Jew wiped his face with his hand, from his forehead all the way down to his beard. Then he brushed a speck of dust from the lapel of his gaberdine, sighed, and turned toward the acacias.

"Where do you think you're going, Pinkus?" called the steward.

"What do you mean, where? To Niemirów. I'm going back to Niemirów."

"What about the gelding?"

"Where Pinkus goes, his horse follows," said the Jew.

"What for?" asked the steward. "I can handle things just as well as Mr. Pilecki. Maybe even better."

"You can never tell in advance," said the Jew. "Is Niemirów at the ends of the earth? When the master's back I'll come again."

"The poor horse'll founder. It's going to be boiling hot."

"A horse like that? You have quite a sense of humor. A horse like that isn't going to founder."

"I couldn't say, since I've not seen him . . . "

The Jew wagged his finger playfully at the steward, turned so the dust rose under his feet, and set off down the path toward the bank of acacias. The steward followed him.

The boy heard their voices growing quieter, and laughed.

That tall, thin Jew in his gaberdine, against the background of the distant fields extending along the shores of the lake, lent character to the whole place. It couldn't be the back of beyond, cut off from the world, since virtually at its threshold the boy had encountered someone who had been part and parcel of his entire life.

Every day, on his way to school, on the busy streets he was surrounded by the same dark bustling throng of dignified old Jews and resolute Jewish teenagers who ran by, pounding the Warsaw cobblestones with their great boots. He liked to watch this world, which was strange and familiar, distant and close at the same time. On Friday afternoons especially, his curiosity drew him to the little stores in the old, half-ruined apartment houses whose windows onto the streets were all open; and above all, it drew him to the people. They were always in uneasy motion, as if energy had built up and was seeking a way out at any cost, as if they were imprisoned by the lack of space in the houses, streets, and stores, and by the evanescence of the opportunities given them by fate. He often thought to himself that in those crowded streets dwelt a premonition of events to come; and his heart shared the unease of those who lived there. They were like birds falling asleep at dusk on window ledges, even in their slumber alert and tense as they awaited another storm. They were restless and talkative; often they went to excess in expressing their feelings in words, gestures, and even looks. But in their eyes he could always see a shadow of fear, as if they were haunted by uncertainty, as if they were unable to shake off a sense of danger . . .

It wasn't only in the eyes of the passersby in dark gaberdines that he noticed that characteristic shadow. It also flickered beneath the eyelids of his schoolmates, boys in white shirts and patterned ties whom the catechist, standing in the doorway at the start of religion classes, would address with a hint of derision:

"Gentlemen of the Judaic faith and Lutherans, you are requested to leave the classroom!"

The three Protestants left their desks unconstrainedly, glad to avoid a tedious lecture on the Catholic God. Besides, the ginger-haired Lutheran pastor would take them under his wing the moment they were in the corridor.

Three other boys, whom the catechist referred to as "gentlemen of the Judaic faith," left the class with a certain reluctance, as if they bore on their shoulders a fearful guilt for the crucifixion of Jesus Christ.

As concerned Jesus, in his childhood the boy had believed He was a Pole, like everyone else. Was there anyone on earth who didn't speak Polish and didn't know the national anthem, "Poland Has Not Perished Yet"? When he was still in kindergarten he had sung carols under the Christmas tree, and from the words it was quite clear that the Virgin Mary had had Baby Jesus in a stable, surrounded by shepherds. Now, where could that have happened if not along the Vistula? Whenever in his shrill child's voice he had sung "Hushaby, little Jesus," in the impenetrable mists of oblivion he saw himself in his cot, against a background of cream-colored wallpaper, in a darkish room where he had indeed spent the first years of his life, and he heard his mother's soporific tones as she repeated: "Hushaby, darling, hush, hush now!"

Looking at the pictures of Baby Jesus, he found in that small chubby face something that resembled his own features, those of the fat little boy in the photograph, with pink cheeks, fingers like sausages, and curly hair that was still thin.

And so Jesus surely had been Polish, born in Poland under the spreading wings of the White Eagle.

When he found out that it wasn't so, at first he had been worried; then he indignantly rejected this new knowledge. Eventually, however, he began to look at pictures of God with a different eye.

He clearly remembered his first impressions of church. Those impressions were keen and terrible. His whole child's person was filled with the rumble of the organ descending from somewhere up above, out of sight. He knelt in the pew; he could feel beneath his knees the hard wood and the cold stone floor. His head was filled with the clamor of the organ pipes, and when he laid a small hand on the front of the pew, he could feel a trembling that passed through the wood. He looked at the altar and saw the massive gold canopy, and below it a host of statues of the saints and the beatified. A little to the side, in a vaulted aisle, Christ hung on the cross.

Christ was not Jesus. For in the boy's mind Jesus was small, blue, and golden, while Christ appeared yellow, dark, and indescribably old. Jesus was an infant lying in a manger, surrounded by joyful shepherds and a band of merry animals, among which one could easily make out an ass, a cow, some sheep, and even a rooster. The Mother of God leaned over Jesus proudly, dressed in peasant's clothes, with a small, sweet, girlish face.

Christ, on the other hand, was a giant with powerful shoulders, loins, thighs, and chest, with a terrible face that expressed a suffering the boy could not understand. Christ was an old man with long hair and a beard. On his head he wore a crown of thorns, from beneath which thick drops of blood ran onto his face. That whole face seemed to abide in a bluish shadow, which filled the boy with dread. The eyes of Christ were closed, while Jesus's tiny eyes were always open and gazing curiously at the world. Christ hung on the cross in a way that was somehow heavy and motionless; and the boy knew that that heaviness and motionlessness indicated death. But at that time he didn't yet know what death was. And so he was afraid of Christ more than he felt sorry for Him.

He didn't recognize Our Lady either. He saw her in dark robes, with an expression of despair on her face. Yet he was most surprised by her hands. They were old and marked with prominent veins; they held onto various objects powerlessly, or sometimes with an awful strength, like talons.

It was only years later that the boy understood that this showed suffering after the loss of her son. Yet that son was no longer a little child but an old, ravaged man pinned to the cross with rusted nails. Everything seemed somehow uncanny to the boy, above all alien and distant . . .

And again several years passed. Then he understood. He slowly forgot about Jesus, whom he had left behind in his childhood room, among the toys he had long ago stopped playing with. Sometimes he took them up again, with that sentimentality and indulgence which usually accompany memories of childhood. And so he also went back to Jesus, and at Christmastime he even enjoyed singing softly by the tree: "Hushaby, little Jesus." But it was never Jesus who was the source of his unease.

Yet when he understood that Christ had died on the cross, for the second time he understood death. From that moment on, looking at the Crucifixion, he felt compassion, gratitude, and dread. He felt compassion for the suffering, he was grateful for that terrible sacrifice that was offered for him, among others, and he dreaded death. He was unable to cross the next threshold of religion, beyond which, he was assured, every person finds a miraculous reconciliation with life and death.

When he first learned that Christ was a Jew, he ran to the nearest church. He looked into the face of the Crucified One. And he saw the dark, curly hair, the dark beard, and that terrible bluish sheen of death beneath the eyelids. He saw a Jew; and he trembled in the depths of his heart, because the certainty that his Polishness was his best pass to heaven had suddenly abandoned him.

He ran feverishly around the churches, staring at the pictures. He was encircled by bearded saints who all looked like Jews. They sat bent over books by the light of tallow candles, and grazed their flocks on the mountainside or amid swirling clouds; most often they were floating in the air, higher and higher, where on a golden throne, in rich and colored vestments, sat God the Father. At His side the boy could see Christ with His gentle, rather melancholy face, and also the Holy Spirit in the form of a white dove fluttering its wings.

God, ancient and mighty, shrouded in silence, seemed to him a rich and powerful Jew; while Christ, with His sorrowful expression and pallid face, seemed a gentle and well-brought-up Jew.

From this time, he felt toward all Jews something like a serene and friendly respect. And even when he had already come to understand something of the complexities of Christianity as set forth by the catechist in his icy voice, when he had grasped the crime of the Crucifixion and the significance of this sacrifice in the Roman Catholic religion, he remained a friend of the Jews. He sometimes thought, aware of the radical nature of such an idea, that the Crucifixion was their own, internal, Jewish affair, which only later, against the will of the high priests of Jerusalem, became a matter for the whole of humanity. After all, it was the Jews whom God had chosen, that His son should be born among them and that they should kill Him on the cross. He must have had some reason for such a decision: He could have sent Baby Jesus not to Bethlehem but to Nowy Targ instead!

Thinking in this way, the boy sometimes felt bitter. As if God had been guilty of treachery or, to put it more mildly, of an oversight. For really, He could have arranged things differently. . . . But then the boy was troubled by further doubts and worries. Was it not better in the long run that God had chosen distant Palestine and the Jewish people, dark, quarrelsome, and restless, for the birthplace of His son? Was everything that happened afterward to Christ not the cause of the sad dispersal of the Jews, and thus of their tribulations, their hardship, their woes, the contempt they so often encountered, the animosity of others that beset them . . . ? Was it not better that God had saved the Poles such experiences by not putting them to the terrible test and the temptation of judging the Savior? And in those Jewish eyes of old and young, even of children, was the shadow of fear, doubt, and unease not a trace of the eternal curse of the heavens? And since, one way or the other, everything began in the Jewish tribe, did these people not deserve a modicum of kindly respect, a well-meaning smile, and fellowship?

He wasn't much interested in his Jewish classmates. It was the others, in their yarmulkes and their gaberdines, huddling together on the narrow alleyways, reciting their prayers in guttural voices by the light of the Sabbath candles; it was precisely because of that obvious otherness that they seemed closer to him, more interesting than those well-behaved boys in smoothly ironed pants and shirts with starched collars. And it was only when the catechist stood by the door of the classroom and they filed out, somewhat embarrassed, that he felt a particular connection with them. Because suddenly, twice a week, at a time marked off in the schedule, there fell upon them the separateness and otherness that they may not have desired at all.

Sometimes he thought that it was simply a sin. But that sin lay on the conscience of the catechist, for he himself could afford the luxury of Samaritanism. When it came down to it, it wasn't such a bad thing . . .

A lack of equilibrium—this was what worried him constantly. He found in himself a certain duality, as if he were suspended between the world within him and that outside him. He was a part of everything around him; of that there was no doubt. But he realized too that he was separate. He wasn't able to reconcile this contradiction. He felt himself to be too weak, too inexperienced, and even unworthy to attempt a solution to such a problem.

When this thought first came to him he was not quite seven years old, and he didn't know that this was called loneliness. Later he found the right word, but it turned out not to be enough to restore his peace of mind.

One evening, in the study, he heard some astonishing words from his father's lips:

"Krzyś, when you grow up you'll be alone. But even today you're a little bit alone, because you have to live in your own way."

So that was what it was all about? No one could exist for him or in his name. He had been given that which existed all around him, and he himself had to bring order to it. What was more, he wasn't able to make use of the experiences of others, as he had conclusively learned from the first moments of his childhood. His mother and father, his schoolmasters and peers could tell him many extremely useful things, but they couldn't teach him the most important lesson: what he should do with himself amid this vast world.

And it was then for the first time, in hope and in despair, that he looked to the heavens. Only there could he find a compass, and only in his contacts with God did he not sense his own isolation.

That day, long before sunset, they went hunting. He felt no excitement as he prepared for this outing. When his father had suggested he could take part in the hunting trip, to begin with he had hesitated. What could be interesting about it?

"You can have your own shotgun and pellets," his father said to encourage him.

Oh, they really didn't know him when it came down to it! The times when he had imagined himself to be a trapper in the wilderness of the Appalachian foothills belonged irrevocably to the past. He had long been bored by stalking big game, by the cries of Indians in the depths of the forest, by scalps and musket shots. He had given up trapping and the fur trade, and had left behind the prairies and saloons of the Wild West; even the sails of drifting brigs on the South China Sea no longer drew him. His father still thought his son was breaking mustangs, whereas in reality he was reading about Saint Francis of Assisi and laboriously climbing the steep path of faith.

That's how it is, he thought; your parents are always be-hind! When I was dreaming of the prairies, they suspected me of love for Prince Józef Poniatowski and bought me an uhlan's *czapka*. I wouldn't play with it. Then my father got angry and accused my mother of spoiling me by indulging too many of my whims. While I always longed for things that were unattainable. And when my yearning was finally satisfied, I was no longer the person they thought I was . . .

And so he accepted without enthusiasm the invitation to join the evening hunting party. They were to take shotguns and hunt the ducks that led their bustling lives in the marshes be-tween the lakes.

There occurred a slight disagreement between the boy's parents, because his mother expressed a desire to take part in the hunt. His father objected firmly.

"My dear," he said, "you're weak, and you catch cold eas-ily. Besides, you talk too much. You won't be able to stay silent more than five minutes."

"You're awful," his mother retorted.

Yet she gave in. At bottom they were both right—his father for objecting, and his mother for yielding.

The preparations for the trip took up the hours after lunch. The clock in the playroom was striking six when the boy heard his father's voice calling him in for a conference.

He went in via the veranda and found himself in this part of the house for the first time. The room was immense, with a disproportionately low ceiling. Three windows opened onto the park, but since ancient trees grew there and the shadows of their leaves lay thick on the walls, a greenish semidarkness prevailed throughout. The playroom was cluttered with furniture. There were two sofas, several upright chairs and armchairs, a small console table with a coping in the form of the afterdeck of a seventeenth-century galleon, escritoires with untold numbers of tiny drawers, and also an oval table, around which the gentlemen were gathered. All the objects in the room were old, damaged, and dusty, as if the place had been locked up for years on end and had never been aired out. On the floor, which was composed of tight-fitting oak boards that were almost completely dried out, lay a carpet. At one time it had probably been the color of ripe cherries, with a pattern in yellow, dark and light blue, and black, but at present it was no longer possible to make out the design. The carpet had worn through in a number of places, uncovering the brown floorboards.

On the wall hung two crossed swords, a flintlock musket with a silver-encrusted butt, and a black boar's head that was also covered with dust. One of the creature's eyes had fallen out.

The gentlemen were sitting at the oval table; bluish columns of cigarette smoke rose over their heads. The boy noticed that they all looked alike. They were wearing green hunting jackets, coarse woolen trousers, and high-topped boots of soft leather laced to their knees, while their faces bore that rather intense and rather amusing expression that men usually assume when they wish to demonstrate especial gravity. They reminded the boy of the engravings from the little books he used to read years ago, laboriously tracing his finger from line to line. They were books about the Emperor Napoleon's grenadiers or the fearless insurgents of 1863. The pictures showed the faces of mustachioed, weather-beaten heroes, faces that were wrinkled from stress and from concentration and that were supposed to testify to their true manliness, which in those books meant steadfastness, a sense of honor, loyalty, and courage.

The boy often wondered how it had happened that since those days, everything had gotten mixed up in the world. The emperor's grenadiers never had wives or daughters. Only occasionally would they have mothers. Their mothers sent them out to do battle for the emperor or for Poland, and then waited patiently for their sons to return home. It sometimes happened that they never did return. Then the mothers would weep, but generally in a darkened room, because they were ashamed of shedding tears for fallen heroes. In those books men were the sole inhabitants of the world. Women appeared only in the background, mostly terrified and frail. They were afraid of the men, yet the men were able to save them from every danger. Then the women would roll their eyes, and the men would twitch their mustaches. And off they would go to fight some more.

In the real world that was all around him, on the other hand, things happened quite differently. Above all, at home the boy heard his mother's voice, not his father's. Wherever he turned his head, everywhere women set the tone for the events that took place. In their presence men tended to be brisk; they moved lightly and with a kind of dancing motion, shaking their heads, clearing their throats, and smiling with a certain submissiveness. And it was only when they were alone that they took on other poses. In the presence of women they sat rather stiffly, leaning forward, ready at any moment for action. The boy had the impression that they were subject to the power of a strained watchfulness, hoping not to transgress against certain obligations that in essence he did not understand. But when they found themselves in the company of their own kind, and they were not in danger of the presence of women, the tension vanished. They sprawled in armchairs, their arms dangling loosely. Cigarettes in their mouths, they slurred their words with a sort of weariness, even when they were talking of matters that seemed important. They would cross their legs, and some of them would rake hooked fingers through their hair or twirl the ends of their mustaches.

There was something astonishing in this change, so abrupt and at the same time so capricious. In the presence of women they manifested softness, elasticity, complaisance even, in combination with the tension that seemed to the boy to be a sense of danger. When the women were not there, on the other hand, they became lazy, calm, and relaxed, and at the same time their faces took on a self-confidence and a certain martial audacity. It was precisely at such moments that they resembled grenadiers and insurgents setting off into battle.

When he entered the playroom, then, he saw before him a troop of stalwart Napoleonic soldiers. They sat round the oval table, puffing away at cigarettes. They were at ease and a little weary, as if their beds had been made up and were inviting them to go to sleep. At the same time their faces expressed resoluteness and a strong will, something both dark and stony, which the boy always associated with the smell of sweat, the neighing of horses, gunsmoke, the moans of the wounded, and the pyramids.

The boy's father was sitting on a sofa, his legs crossed; his calves in the tight riding boots looked like those of the stone faun that stood on the plinth in the garden. Next to him, lolling in an armchair, his legs stretched out in front of him, a cigarette in the corner of his mouth, and his eyes half-closed as if he were dozing, sat Major Kurtz, their traveling companion from Warsaw. Pilecki, in an unbuttoned army shirt, the most suntanned of them all, with a wrinkled neck against which the whitish strip of the collar of his jacket stood out like a scar, sat astride a chair as if it were a horse. In front of him, leaning against the arm of the chair, stood a shotgun, the barrel of which he held in place with his fingers. Malinowski, the corpulent, balding steward, occupied a place on the other sofa. He seemed engrossed in the Sisyphean task of stuffing back the reddish tufts of horsehair that were poking out from the torn upholstery. Right by the window, on a hard stool, sat the gamekeeper, whose name was Łoś, a chubby-faced, still youngish man with light straw-colored hair and mustache, who was dressed in a worn and stained forest ranger's uniform. He was the only one wearing stiff farmer's boots spattered with dried mud. In his right hand, which was bent outward like a seashell, he held a glowing cigarette. On the floor at his feet lay a metal box containing tobacco and wafer-thin cigarette papers.

The boy sat on a chair near the gamekeeper. They exchanged glances. The gamekeeper nodded in greeting. Pilecki said:

"So Krzyś'll go with you, Seweryn?"

The boy's father replied:

"I'm not sure . . ."

"I can go on my own," said the boy.

"Best not," said Pilecki. "Hunting's not a game."

"That's right," put in his father.

"I'll take the young gentleman with me," said Łoś, the gamekeeper.

"Splendid," said the boy's father. The boy had the impression that his father was relieved. He wasn't surprised. His father adored hunting. In every free moment during the hunting season, he was prepared to undertake exhausting journeys just so as to be able to spend a few hours wandering through the woods with a shotgun on his arm. His tiring life in Warsaw intensified his longing for solitude in nature.

"Mr. Łoś," said Pilecki, "tell us which way we'll go."

"I think, Captain," said Łoś, "that we'll go down through Zagaje to the marshes, and then we'll split up. Maybe you could head in the direction of Leniwe . . . " He paused, uncertain whether his suggestion was acceptable.

"I'd be glad to go toward Leniwe," said Pilecki. "We can go together, Seweryn!"

"Excellent," agreed the boy's father.

"Major, if you will, you can pass through the alder woods down to the bank of the Sucharek. There are grebes there on the river."

"I know," said Major Kurtz. "I used to hunt down there last summer."

"Exactly, Major," the gamekeeper went on, pleased. "You know the Sucharek. We've been there before. And perhaps Mr. Malinowski and the young gentleman and I could make for Duże, eh? Because if my memory serves me correctly, Major, you like most of all to hunt alone."

"Mr. Malinowski won't be in my way," said Kurtz.

The steward broke off from stuffing the horsehair back in and murmured:

"No, no . . . I'll stick with Mr. Łoś . . . "

"Perfect," concluded Pilecki. "So you and I head for Leniwe, Seweryn, the major to the Sucharek, and the others toward Duże."

All of a sudden he waved his hand.

"That won't do," he said. "What about the dogs? My dear Mr. Malinowski, you'll go with the major after all. Saba will go with you. She doesn't know the major."

"That's true," grunted Kurtz. "I'll be happy to have Mr. Malinowski's company."

"Splendid," put in the boy's father.

"Łoś, you can take Kajtek, and I'll have Julita. All right?" said Pilecki.

"Of course, Captain Pilecki." The gamekeeper nodded with alacrity.

"It's time, it's time," said the boy's father and rose from the sofa. His movements were springy; he was filled with a strange energy. Everyone stood up, and, shuffling their feet, they headed for the door that gave onto the veranda.

"Are we coming back separately or what?" asked Kurtz.

"We'll see how things work out," answered Pilecki. "We ought to be back an hour after sunset. Supper will be waiting."

"I should hope so," muttered the boy's father. "A good supper and a glass of juniper vodka."

"I daresay that can be found too," said Pilecki.

The gentlemen laughed.

One after another they went out onto the veranda; then they walked down the avenue of hornbeams to the gates of the park. The sun was hot; the shadows of leaves danced on the ground. There was a smell of water, greenery, and olden times.

From the gate they could hear the barking and whining of the dogs. As they drew closer, the boy saw three pointers held on short, strained leashes by the wiry old countryman who had carried the lamps into the dining room the previous evening. When the dogs saw the hunters they set about yelping with joy. The countryman bowed awkwardly and somewhat unthinkingly, as if he were in a hurry all of a sudden; then he handed the dogs to Malinowski. He in turn passed the leashes to the other hunters. As had been agreed, Pilecki took the bitch called Julita, lean and highly strung, with a slender snout and reddish eyes. The other bitch, Saba, who had a touch of the mongrel in her and who was bigger and stronger than Julita, yet lacking in grace, went with Malinowski. The gamekeeper got Kajtek, an old hand and a joker with a resolute and slightly sardonic face. Kajtek was not a thoroughbred pointer either; he had an admixture of setter in him, and from his forehead a coarse curl of hair stuck out roguishly.

And so they set off, the dogs on taut leashes ahead of the men, and the men silent and intent. After a short while they separated at the marshes. They said not a word to one another; each turned in his own direction, bidding farewell to his companions with a gesture and a glance.

The gamekeeper went in front, preceded by the dog. The boy followed him at a short distance. They entered a hazel wood. Here the ground was sodden; the path twisted between patches of springy moss. Among the trees there was a still, languid, humid heat, despite the fact that evening was approaching.

Łoś walked in a sprightly fashion, without looking back. The pointer took ever shorter and shallower breaths; the collar was tight around his throat, and he tugged at the tightly stretched leash, infused with the hunting instinct. The dog's tension gradually infected the boy. He placed his feet less cautiously, and once or twice he made a splash as he strayed from the path.

Suddenly there was a whirring among the hazel trees; a group of ducks rose skyward, then they disappeared amid the greenery, and silence fell once more.

At last they came out onto open ground, on the shore of the lake, which was densely overgrown with willows. Now the gamekeeper loosed the dog. The pointer moved forward, his nose to the ground. His body all at once acquired grace and delicacy; his step was easy, light, almost soundless. He disappeared into the willows; they heard the plash of water, and again, all of a sudden, like exploding shrapnel, some ducks scattered upward. A flock of them rose in a heavy, trailing flight with a resonant flapping of wings, then in a twinkling they aligned themselves in an amazingly straight line and glided toward the middle of the lake.

The gamekeeper stood still, slowly removed the shotgun from his shoulder, then sought the trail again and resumed his march with a lazy step. He didn't even try to take aim; it was decidedly too late for that.

"Who'd've thought they were lurking so close," he muttered.

So they went on, at a distance from the water, going round the willows in a gentle arc. The dog ran right along the shoreline, watchful, silent, taut as a violin string. Suddenly the gamekeeper whispered meaningfully:

"Is this your first time hunting ducks, young sir?"

The boy nodded.

"You should know that shooting at a bird that's on the water isn't done," said Łoś. He spoke oddly, as if he were afraid of offending his companion, yet intent on his mission as a mentor.

"I see," said the boy. "Why can't you shoot them on the water?"

"At those times the duck isn't moving," said Łoś. "It's easy to hit it. The bird doesn't have a chance on the water, and you have every chance. It's not worthy of a hunter."

"I understand," said the boy. "So only when it's flying in the air?"

"When it's in flight," confirmed the gamekeeper. "The dog will set the bird, that is, it'll flush it out from where it's hidden in the willows, and it'll fly upward. Then you have to give it a moment to rise up a little, and only then shoot at it. It's not right to do it earlier, right over the water, because then the bird has a heaviness about it, it's not gotten as high as it needs, and it doesn't stand a chance of getting away. After, when it's gliding, the chances are more even. You'll either hit it or you won't."

"I get it," the boy said in a whisper.

"And fire ahead of the duck. Anyway, I'll show you."

"All right."

All at once he had lost any desire to go hunting. The thought occurred to him that there was a great foolishness and baseness in all this. First they order him to stick to the rules of the game, so as not to deny the ducks a chance of survival, then they tell him to kill them and expect him to shoot straight. What nonsense! When it came down to it, why had they come here? If they wanted to shoot these wretched birds, they should try to be efficient, to surprise the bird at rest in the willows, entangled even, and let rip with both barrels, a sure thing. If on the other hand they believed that the duck should have a chance of survival, they should sit in the playroom or on the veranda overlooking the lawn and talk about politics and travel. The whole tale of equal chances for hunter and animal was a deceitful prevarication. They want to appear not as murderers but as gallant knights who have overcome the enemy. There was duplicity in this, because no duck had ever pecked a hunter to death.

Once again he recalled the illustrations from his childhood books, and he felt cheated. Those grenadiers and insurgents had a higher purpose and were exposed to real danger. They went to war against armed men; they killed and were killed. And the pioneers on the prairies of Texas? How many times in the cinema had he seen their corpses bristling with Indian arrows! The wagon train, formed into a circle, thundered with gunfire and was enveloped in smoke like a besieged fortress, while the Indians galloped round, dispatching a hail of arrows in the direction of the wagons. Many a trapper dropped dead, hit by a shaft that lodged in his chest or neck. Sometimes the pioneers' wagons went up in flames; ammunition ran low, the ring of Indians drew closer and closer. And then, from afar, came the ringing sound of a bugle, and columns of cavalry streamed down from the hills. Yet on the battlefield there were left the motionless bodies of both vanquished and victors. This had some meaning. It was barbaric and cruel, but it had meaning . . .

Here, on the other hand, amid the watery hazel woods and the willows, the battle was nothing but a fantasy of the men in green jackets and high laced boots. They crept up to the defenseless game like robbers, then at the last minute they required observance of some dumb code that they'd set up to satisfy the principle of fair play and to stifle the pangs of their consciences. It was a subterfuge on their part, a coarse and laughable deception that they elevated to the rank of a moral principle. In this way, they turned their cruel recreation into a noble and truly manly venture worthy of courageous and risk-loving people. If they had at least been hunting a tiger with spears, like in prehistoric times. . . . In those days people were struggling for their existence; to survive, they had to kill big game in the forests. They returned to their settlements wounded and weak, but with a sense of a duty properly fulfilled, because on their shoulders they bore food for the women and children. A number of them remained forever in the backwoods, mauled to death by wild animals.

Today, what had once been a necessity of life they had turned into an amusement. But they wouldn't admit it! And so they contrived deceptions and subterfuges, they imposed upon themselves ridiculous restrictions that were supposed to attest to their sense of justice and respect for their adversary. But there no longer was any adversary or any justice. There was nothing but the despicable entertainment of bad, stupid, powerful men, in which defenseless creatures fell victim to them.

The boy drew up suddenly. He stood against a background of mottled greenery; the branches of the hazel trees cast shadows across his face. The sun was shining just above the tops of the hornbeams and the young oaks, and was dropping slowly toward the waters of the lake. A gray cloud, which seemed to be smoldering in the heat of the day, passed lazily across the sky. The pointer stood stock-still, its right forepaw raised and its nose turned to the mild breeze that was ruffling the willows. The gamekeeper took a step and rested his foot on a fallen log. And all at once everything froze, as sometimes happens in the cinema when the projector breaks. At such times there is a tension-filled moment, then the audience begins to call out. But while that one fleeting second of silence and stillness lasts, something extraordinary happens. It is as if the nature of the world undergoes a startling transformation.

The boy stood still as a statue, lifeless, bitter, desperate. He knew that an instant later the world would begin to move again, so that the murder could be carried out. At this moment he hated the gamekeeper, himself, his father, all people; he even hated the dog, who remained in his bizarre pose, as if he were no longer a dog, as if he were no longer a creature irrevocably fated to die but an instrument, a part of the mechanism of this terrible, mindless destruction.

Suddenly, among the willows there came two quick, dull smacks; the stalks swayed and parted, revealing a sheet of livid water. A number of ducks flapped their wings, and in the sun's rays the drops of water sparkled with a yellow and blue light. A clatter of wings against water exploded all about, ricocheted off the hazel woods, and bounced back across the lake in a wet echo. The pointer leaped into the marsh; the ducks rose ponderously into the air, one, two, three, four of them. . . . They flew with a disturbing ease, stretched out with fear. All at once they cut across the sun like a black bisector.

Then a shot rang out, and after it a second. The boy saw the gamekeeper. He was standing in a curious position, one leg resting on a fallen tree trunk, the other held behind him as if he were lame. His left hand supported the stock of the gun; the right was bent at the trigger. The butt was pressed between his shoulder and his cheek as if it were growing out of him, as if it constituted an extension of his body. A delicate, bluish smoke was rising and blowing away.

"Now!" called the gamekeeper. "Now!"

The duck he had hit flew lower; its entire body spun, while its wings, spread wide, stopped flapping.

The boy, instinct with something alien, evil, and incomprehensible that came from outside him yet controlled his existence utterly, lifted the shotgun and aimed. He thought to himself that he should take aim without hurrying. He mustn't miss; he should fire in front of the duck to intercept the line of its flight. For a split second he held the bird's body in his sights; then he moved the barrel slightly to the right and pulled the trigger. There was a crash. He pulled again. Another crash. The shots sounded flat, wet, hideous. The duck, whose wing was just crossing the orb of the sun, fluttered as if caught in a net; the hail of shot threw it to the side, and it dropped off course, turned in a half circle as if trying to get back to the safety of its original line of flight, then suddenly, with a swinging movement, it fell slowly and languidly to the waters of the lake.

"Good shot!" cried the gamekeeper.

The pointer had already emerged from the reeds by the shore, carrying in its mouth the first dead duck. The gamekeeper took it from him, threw it down at his feet, and said excitedly:

"Fetch, Kajtek! Fetch!"

The dog went back into the willows.

The body of the bird the boy had shot was floating on the water. He watched as the pointer swam in that direction, took hold of the dead bird in its mouth with great delicacy, maybe even with a slight distaste, nimbly turned around, and swam back to the bank. He watched the dog make its way through the willows and come out onto dry land, bring the duck to the gamekeeper, crouch and breathe noisily, moving its stump of a tail agitatedly. He watched the gamekeeper toss the second duck to the ground, then, smiling, hang the shotgun on a hazel branch, take the little tin from his pocket, open it carefully so as not to spill its precious contents, sit on a log, and set about rolling a cigarette. He watched the white paper in the game-keeper's fingers fill with strands of tobacco, swell, and be neatly rolled up, then rise to the level of his lips, from between which there emerged his tongue, pink, slippery, and deft; he watched the tongue move slowly along the rolled-up paper, in coordi-nation with fast, precise movements of the fingers. He watched the cigarette shift to the corner of the gamekeeper's mouth, where the upper lip was encircled by the crescent of his straw-colored mustache, and he watched the gamekeeper's fingers, which looked like fat, restless bugs, take hold of a match and rub it against the side of the matchbox; then he watched the little flame ignite, yellow with a crimson core, and rise upward to light the cigarette. He watched the paper slowly catch fire and turn red at the very tip, while brown strips crept toward the gamekeeper's mouth.

He watched all this and felt he was dying. And when his gaze dropped downward, he saw two small, helpless birds upon the trampled grass. The wing of one, its feathers bristling, disproportionately large, stuck up like a black hand reaching out from a freshly filled-in grave.

The gamekeeper was enjoying his cigarette. The smoke formed a halo around his head. There was a smell of decomposition all around. The gamekeeper extended a leg, touched one of the ducks with the tip of his boot and said:

"They're fat ones. The two of them won't fit on one baking dish."

"I won't eat them," said the boy. He had a lump in his throat. He was disgusted by his own hands, his own voice. He was disgusted by everything.

"It'll be good meat. Tender," said the gamekeeper.

"Give me mine, Mr. Łoś," said the boy.

"That's your due," said the gamekeeper.

He picked up one of the ducks.

"It's heavy," he said. "A fat one."

He was holding it by the neck; its head hung down inertly, and its yellow and pink bill was cadaverous and terrible.

The boy was about to take the bird, but he became scared.

"I won't eat it," he repeated, and turned his head away. He felt despair and powerlessness. I'll bury it, he thought suddenly. I'll dig it a grave and bury it.

"A bird's a bird and a person's a person," said the gamekeeper suddenly, looking askance at the boy. "That's just how things are, young sir. We need to be getting on . . . "

He rose from the log, brushed off the seat of his pants, put the tin away carefully, and slung the gun over his right arm.

"A bird's a bird," he repeated. His face wore a sad expression. It looked like the dead bird that he had hung from his belt.

"So what are we going to do with that?" he asked, indicating the other bird.

The boy walked away without a word. The gamekeeper tied the second duck to a ringlet on his belt, clicked to the pointer, threw the butt of his cigarette into the reeds, and followed the boy.

The sun was dropping ever more abruptly. To the west the blue sky first turned purple, then took on a red color. The water glistened among the reeds. A great black beetle alighted on a hazel leaf. Somewhere on the opposite shore of the lake a shot rang out. It hadn't yet died away when further shots followed. The gamekeeper said quietly:

"Your dad must have come upon a flock. And Captain Pilecki. The captain has good luck."

Then once again he repeated in a plaintive, old woman's tone of voice:

"A bird's just a bird. That's all there is to it . . . "

That evening supper went on for a long time. The dining room was lit up with a number of lamps set in a circle on the dresser and the table. Fish and meat were served, then cakes and dessert. The gentlemen drank juniper vodka, the ladies wine. Everyone was merry; the men related their experiences during the hunt, while the two old ladies in their black shawls gave out delighted cries.

The boy's mother seemed to him less beautiful than usual; her look conveyed boredom and a little irritation. He thought to himself that quite simply she couldn't bear not to be the center of attention. When the talk was of the hunt, she was silent. She ate little, and her smile was somewhat forced; her thick, dark lashes at times covered her eyes, and at such moments her face assumed an expression of bitterness.

The boy's father was radiant. He gulped down his food, heedless of its taste, utterly engrossed in his story. He and Pilecki had had quite an adventure: As they had been tracking down a flock of grebes, they had fallen into the marsh, and it had taken them almost three-quarters of an hour to get out. They had been saved by a tree that had been blown down in a storm. They slid up the slippery trunk onto firmer ground; but they were covered in mud from head to foot, so they had had to give up the idea of any more hunting and had gone to bathe in the lake. Earlier on, however, they had already bagged a number of ducks, so the hunt had been successful.

Major Kurtz brought back seven fat, handsome birds. He had the right to consider himself the victor; yet when he heard the story told by the boy's father, he seemed a little dispirited that fate had denied him such a fine adventure.

Over the roast one of the old ladies, whom they called Aunt Cecylia, recounted a story from her youth. It transpired that she too had almost drowned in a marsh, when as a young lady she had been traveling by wagon all the way to Niemirów to fetch the doctor. It happened one night in March. That evening someone in the manor had accidentally cut his shin with an ax, and it was necessary to summon the healer. Miss Cecylia's father was not at home at the time, while the steward lay drunk in his bedchamber; so the enterprising young woman decided she would bring help herself. However, that night there came a thaw, which could not have been foreseen. The young lady had taken a shortcut across the iced-over marshes, confident that she would reach Niemirów without any problem. Suddenly, under the weight of the horse and cart the ice gave way; there was a terrible gurgling sound under the surface and the cart began to sink into the shifting marsh. The horse was stuck up to his hindquarters, unable to move, and began whinnying in fear. The moon shone indifferently; all about there was silence and the soft rustle of the woods. There was no hope. Aunt Cecylia clambered out of the cart and, by an extraordinary stroke of luck, found a strong branch within arm's reach. She climbed up the young oak and sat like an owl in the leafless top of the tree, wearing a short mantle, a skirt, and a jacket lined with rabbit's fur. In front of her eyes the horse, neighing in desperation, sank into the marsh with the wagon. Before daybreak the frost set in again. The young lady shivered on her branch, preparing herself for death. She was haunted, she said, by the reproachful eye of the horse, who had perished in the moonlight, helplessly immobilized till he had disappeared in the billowing, greenish depths of the mosses, water, and weeds of the marsh. At sunrise Miss Cecylia was found by people from Nałęcz who had been sent out to look for her. Afterward she spent three days in bed, being treated with juices and mustard compresses.

"I almost died," squeaked the old lady, and took a sip of wine.

"And the farmhand?" asked the boy's mother.

"Farmhand? What farmhand? I was alone on the marsh."

"The man who'd injured himself with an ax?"

"He recovered," replied the old lady grudgingly, somewhat offended.

Then Major Kurtz told the tale of how as a child he had almost drowned in a river. He too had been rescued at virtually the last moment, by fishermen. In fact, whoever had been in danger had always been saved in the nick of time. Pilecki, for instance, had used up his last bullet and was preparing for death when relief had come. Even Malinowski, the steward, when he had been set upon by thieves in Warsaw, had already felt the blade of the knife against his throat when a passing detachment of soldiers had scared away his assailants.

Listening to these confidences, the boy was thinking lazily how it never happened that an adventure lasted less time, or that its course was less dramatic. It was always the last bullet, the last moment, and the last chance. The person who was being attacked always saw the flash of the knife and felt the blade under their chin or on the back of their neck; relief always came right when the ammunition had run out, and the tree extended its saving branches as the victim felt the water rushing into their mouth. Does fate always arrange accidents in real life in accordance with what happens in books, at the cinema, or on the stage? Those soldiers who in the movie are always walking down another street when they hear the last cry of the person being assaulted and turn back at a run: In real life are they ever walking down the right street? Is the relief always so sluggish that it arrives to save the last survivor instead of appearing a quarter of an hour earlier and coming to the aid of the whole unit of its comrades in arms? And finally, do the fishermen, seeing the boy swimming, not draw his attention to the whirlpools but instead occupy themselves in idle conversation, hurrying to the rescue only when the child has already disappeared into the foaming depths?

Or maybe it was just that experiences related at a lavishly provided table, in the bright light of lamps, in a secure house, and in pleasant company, took on a literary suggestiveness because only literature can arouse sympathy, create suspense, and heighten attention, whereas life itself, in its indeterminate shape, leaves listeners bored and indifferent?

The boy stared at the company gathered around the table. The faces, with the exception of his mother's, were all rosy, eyes shining, gestures somewhat excitable. Even Monika, who was sitting at a distance, partly in shadow, seemed to the boy to be utterly engrossed in the stories, as if she were envious because of all the dangers, perils, and miraculous escapes that had not yet happened to her.

But the most attractive face was that of the venerable Miss Cecylia. While she was telling the tale of her rescue on the marsh, her eyes glistened, and her wrinkled cheeks lost their bluish whiteness. Later, as she listened to the others, she wore a slightly derisive smile on her lips, but curiosity lurked in her eyes. The boy thought to himself that the old lady didn't believe any of the adventures except her own, but she longed to see how other people would resolve their stories and how they would modulate the drama of the situation. Miss Cecylia seemed quite simply to be reading someone else's book. She treated the plot with a certain scorn, because her own was better and more exciting, but she couldn't control her avid inquisitiveness.

The old woman's mouth was twisted in a slightly sarcastic smile, exposing her toothless gums. Her watery little eyes rested with a mocking attentiveness on Kurtz, Pilecki, and Malinowski in turn. Her small hands lay still on the tablecloth, though from time to time her thin fingers brushed up crumbs of bread that had spilt from her plate.

At one moment, as the major was describing his near drowning in the river, which had ended so fortunately, Miss Cecylia interrupted him with the words:

"What was that? What was that again?"

"I felt that in another moment I'd no longer be able to breathe," repeated the major, somewhat thrown off course, since the sequence of his story had been mixed up. "And it was just then . . . "

"I understand, my dear sir," said the old lady. "Come along then, get on with it."

Now she could drown with him, able to breathe easily in the large, cool room. And it was at this second that the boy was overcome with an overwhelming feeling of compassion. He looked at the old face, the old neck, and the old hands of this woman, who for over seventy years had climbed the steep stairs in this house with her short steps, in the evening carrying a candle or a kerosene lamp above her head. He saw her, stooped and weak, crossing the lawn or walking along a path in the park, entering the manor kitchen, which was lined from floor to ceiling with clay pots and jugs, arranging bouquets of wild flowers and putting them in vases in the playroom, or watering the vegetable patch in the garden behind the barns. He thought to himself that she had always, even at the time of her adventure on the marsh, been old and decrepit, half deaf and half blind, that the faintest breeze from the lake could knock her over, that she could get sunburned from the slightest March sunshine peeping out from behind clouds. She was as fragile as glass, light as a feather, tiny as a seed, thin as a reed, wrinkled as a nut, cold as ice. She was old, old, old; and it was this that suddenly terrified him!

He looked at Monika, whose small face was in shadow, outside the circle of the kerosene lamps. He looked at his mother, leaning toward the major as he spoke. Then he looked back at Miss Cecylia. So this was life, this was what it was about, about a perpetual loss, a drying up, a crumbling. There remains only a hollowed-out, dried-up little bug. Old woman, old woman—what on earth does that mean? It occurred to him that it was a mistake, a defect in the language, which is incapable of expressing the whole truth. How could she be a woman if she was so old? Was anything left that could be called womanly? In that countryman who brought in the lighted lamps and held the dogs on their leashes by the gateway to the park, was there any manliness left? Both of them, he and Miss Cecylia, were old, and their age had branded them with a mark that excluded womanliness and manliness. Both of them were shriveled, extinguished, hollow. They lacked strength, and as they moved, in their empty innards you could hear the dull sound of beggars' rattles.

That was exactly it! Unsatiated poverty was rattling about in them; they were demanding alms. They were begging for a look, a word, a gesture; because everything they possessed came from outside them, it was a gift from the world, which superciliously dispensed crumbs from its own surplus. They existed thanks to the condescension of others; they were warmed by the warmth of others, protected by the strength of others, and they lived the lives of others; even their fears were borrowed from others' fears, their cares the reflection of the cares of others, and their joy mirrored the joy of others.

And they had only one thing left to call their own—death! So they thought about it, prepared for it, jealously guarded their contact with it, for it was all their fortune, their sacred possession. And only they could talk with death. . . . When Miss Cecylia was telling the tale of her adventure on the marsh, even though the listeners didn't believe everything, a chill ran down their spines and their hair stood on end from fear. Whereas when the major, Pilecki, or the steward were talking, there was an amiable sense of relief around the table. As Miss Cecylia described the eye of the dying horse, her expression was intense, tiny, dry; yet a soft radiance infused her yellowish forehead and pale cheeks. At that time she could see what others could not: She saw the dying of the horse, terrible, isolated, and alone in the world; a dying that she had already come to terms with, that she had already trained to her own ends, while the others around the table listened to the story as if it were a fairy tale.

And so, thought the boy, not everything has been taken from her after all! She has lost her strength and her purpose in life, and the juices of existence have dried up within her, leaving ruins lit by the pale glow of the moon. Yet in this frail and empty carapace of a body there is not just a resounding emptiness, but there also dwells something great and mysterious, which none of us knows or can comprehend: a holy reconciliation with departure and with leave-taking.

Poor, old lady, he thought. Poor, old lady.

And he felt a great tenderness toward her, and toward the countryman from the stables. And he thought about his grandmother, who right now was probably extinguishing the light and settling down to sleep in distant Warsaw. He was struck by a terrible, painful longing for his grandmother. His throat was dry and he felt moisture under his eyelids. He closed his eyes and imagined his grandmother in her casket, in the flickering golden light of candles. Then, all at once his thoughts and images became mixed up. He saw God looking down sternly on the duck that had been killed. He recalled the cold of the shotgun butt against his right cheek, the metallic click of the trigger, the bang of the shot. He opened his eyes wide, looked at the old woman across the table, at his mother, and at Monika. Life and death, he thought. Life and death. It's terrible . . .

Cake and sugared fruits had just been served.

Over dessert the company talked of war: not of the last war, but of the one that might come. Opinions were divided. Major Kurtz expressed an optimistic outlook.

"The Germans would have to be mad to risk war on two fronts in the present situation," he said.

"The Germans went mad once before," murmured Pilecki. "What do you think about all this, Seweryn?"

Pilecki was always unsure of himself and sought support from elsewhere, as if he lacked the strength on his own. The boy's father shrugged; with his fingertips he crumbled a piece of cake on his plate.

"Hitler is a terrible man," he said, "but the Germans are a cultured nation. And they're known for their common sense."

"If I might say something," put in Malinowski. "I know them. I was taken prisoner by the Germans. I have to admit . . .

it was clean and orderly, the treatment was humane. But Hitler is an entirely different kettle of fish."

"I don't deny," said Pilecki, "that Germans are often decent people. Yet one hears unbelievable things. Could anyone have ever imagined that the Germans would be arresting completely innocent people? They've set up concentration camps, where apparently they're keeping Socialists, Communists, even Catholics. It's beyond comprehension, my friends. And freedom of speech is out. Is that possible in Germany? They had the best newspapers in the world, everyone wrote whatever they wanted, and now all of a sudden . . . "

Major Kurtz gave a sour laugh.

"The world moves forward," he said. "Right into the trap!"

He wore a tired expression; all his vigor had evaporated, leaving only a healthy red color in his cheeks. Miss Cecylia nodded her little head. Her younger sister, whose name was Róża, silent and gray as a mouse, stirred from a doze and said quietly:

"The time has come."

There was no way of knowing whether she meant that the time had come for the world as it headed straight into the murderous trap, or whether she had decided that the hour was late.

The boy's mother began to describe a reception in Berlin a few years before.

"Can you imagine," she said, turning to the major, "that I was given a bouquet of light blue roses! They have a special nursery there where they apply some sort of chemicals. The roses were gorgeous, but they had no scent."

"Well, I never," said Malinowski. "The Germans are clever folks."

"It's just as well," said Pilecki, "that we're so far away. They'd never get as far as Nałęcz. It's such a long way . . ."

"They came this far during the last war," said Malinowski. "And much further too—"

"You can't make that comparison," said the boy's father. "Those were completely different times, there was a different balance of powers. Besides, to be perfectly honest, I don't believe in this war. One has to keep one's nerves in check."

"But what if it happens after all?" murmured Pilecki.

"Then we'll fight," said the boy's father decisively. Major Kurtz nodded. The boy's mother sighed. Miss Cecylia nodded her head again. Her sister Róża had fallen asleep. Monika smiled at the boy. The boy smiled at her.

He thought to himself that he had wasted a whole day in foolishness, instead of getting to know this girl. Tomorrow, he thought, I'll talk with her. She's so pretty.

Then he thought further that the war which the adults were talking about did not interest him in the slightest. He felt heavy and tired. I wish they'd stop talking already, he said to himself, and go to bed!

Through the open window the wind blew into the room the scent of herbs, mowed clover, and mature honey. The moon cast a pale light onto the waters of the lake. A tiny cloud moved slowly across the tops of the hornbeams and the poplars.

The boy lay in bed and couldn't get to sleep. First he thought about the hunt, then he went over the conversation at supper and imagined the coming war. Finally he thought about his father, and about how he loved him very much. He wanted to be like his father. Yet not entirely, for he rejected certain details and altered others. For instance, that whole inconsistency in his manner.

His father was a strict and demanding person. He was known for his taciturnity; he lived in his study like a badger in his den, entrenched in rigid domestic habits that even his wife did not dare to disturb. He dressed neatly though not stylishly, and had a preference for dull colors. He smoked cigars or fat cigarettes with a mouthpiece, ate always with a knife and fork and never with his hands, and walked erect with a measured step, as if he were afraid that any more abrupt movement would diminish the dignity of his person.

In his study he would sit in a rocking chair, and he seemed to enjoy its monotonous creak. His desk, which was always tidy, was in his absence kept locked with a key, which he hung on a long gilt chain attached to his watch fob. Every evening he would take from the drawer a thick notebook and record in it all the expenses he had incurred during the day. But this did not testify in the least to a frugal lifestyle, much less to a systematicness of thoughts and actions. It was not that the boy's father was a pedant but that he very much wanted to be; and he compensated for the imperfections that arose from his disordered, excitable nature with trifles that could pass for absolution. At bottom, he was a gregarious person who was fond of conversation. But a painful thorn had lodged in him. He came from a simple family; he had gained an education with great difficulty, at the price of self-denial, in hardship. He had probably not been an especially brilliant or able young man, and so learning had come to him with an effort; it had cost him great pains to scrape through all his exams in school and in college, and he had experienced many failures. This had made him stubborn, rigid, and unsure of himself. Among people with the same education and social position as his he probably felt himself to be worth more, for while they had achieved everything effortlessly, thanks to their refinement, intelligence, and upbringing, he had climbed to these peaks from great depths. He didn't like it when people made fun of learning, titles, or high office. His own had cost him too much for him to scorn them. His childhood had left him with a timidity toward the outside world, which later became his world. And so he took everything terribly seriously, with gravity and solemnity, in which he resembled the peasants from whom he had come. He had no sense of humor, nor of lightheartedness, nor easy behavior. He was unyielding, demanding, stubborn, and closemouthed. Yet in the depths of his heart he was probably aware that this shell chafed against him. He had moments of relaxation, when his laughter could be heard in his study, a little too loud and too merry. Once in a while he crooked his elbow, and at such times he occasionally drank too much.

His attitude to the boy was quite bizarre. "Study," he would say, "because I want to be proud of you."

He regarded learning as the key to all the secrets of life, and also saw in it the opportunity to rise above mediocrity. He was a fanatic when it came to learning; in this matter he wouldn't tolerate idleness, levity, or a lack of willingness. Nor was he satisfied when the boy found school too easy. He believed that education required effort, and if one achieved results too readily, then clearly it wasn't of any great value!

In these issues there was a long-standing disagreement between the boy's father and his mother. For his mother had a volatile mind and a relaxed approach to life; she satisfied herself with what was easy and pleasant, and avoided any sacrifice like the plague.

"I was born to be entertained," she would say openly.

This his father could never understand. For he divided his life into work and rest, as the Bible taught. True, he had never been a religious man; he didn't attend church, and he conducted his business with the Lord God with great discretion. But peasant blood flowed in his veins, and because of this he remained conservative. He treated work with respect, with a certain idolatrous humility; whereas amusements that brought no concrete results in life seemed to him quite simply stupid and harmful. He never went to the movies; he was so reluctant and slow to go to the theater that he probably never made it there either. Even in his hours of rest he continued his learning: He would read books from which he could draw new information, and he learned foreign languages; or he would simply go on long, tiring walks to maintain his health.

The boy's parents loved each other very much, perhaps precisely because they were so different, and in essence so alien to each other . . .

The boy's mother had received an indifferent education, but she was experienced in the ways of the world and sure of herself because of her beauty and her husband's position; she was able to shine in any company. She was the only one whom the boy's father forgave for that! He scorned other such people, because he was irritated by the shallowness of their minds, the vapidity of their prattle, and the easiness of their lives. He loved the boy's mother above all else, and so was probably gratified that she drew the attention of every companion with her charm and her good manners. But his view of women had been developed on the basis of extremely meager and limited observation, for other than his own wife he had only passing contact with them. Thus, he believed that women were harebrained, foolish, and frivolous, that they could not be relied upon or trusted, and that there was no hope they would ever grow wiser. In this too he was the conservative peasant; while above all he had begun to uncover the most profound secret, the essence of which was that he was afraid of women, because of his shyness and want of experience.

The boy sensed this, as he was more mature than his father by a whole era! And it may have been just because of this that more and more often he thought of him with affection; it seemed to him that life had treated his father harshly, and had never granted him that unrest, anxiety, and joyous expectation which the boy was feeling right now, as he looked at the moonlit night outside the window, at the silver tops of the hornbeams and the poplars, and leaned his whole being toward the future.

The sunlight filtered through into the depths of the lake. All around there was a yellowish glow, against which rocked the shadows of the stalks immersed in the water. Pebbles and fragments of shells glittered on the bottom.

The lake was chilly; he felt the delicate pinch of cold on his skin. When he rose from the water the heat struck him. The sun was high in a cloudless sky. Along the shore there stretched a wall of greenery, swaying in the breeze.

He came out of the water and shook himself like a dog. The girl was sitting on the shingle; she had dipped her feet in the silt of the shore. She was wearing a thin dress that clung to her body. She said:

"You swim well. But why do you splash around like that?"

"Come into the water. Don't be afraid."

"I don't like to," she retorted.

He sat by her, on a rock. The sun warmed his neck and back. He could sense himself drying, and he felt good. He touched the girl's sleeve with his fingertips.

"What's that?"

"A dress."

"I know. But what material is it made of?"

"I guess it's cotton," she answered.

"Why 'I guess'? Don't you know about these things?"

"No. I'm not interested in dresses."

"I know why you don't want to go swimming. You don't have anything to wear."

"Don't be silly," she said unwillingly. "I can swim naked if I feel like it."

In spite of the heat he felt his cheeks burning. He looked at the girl in disbelief.

"You could? Tell me the truth!"

She shrugged, and smiled.

"This is the country," she said. "The middle of nowhere. You can walk all the way round the lake and you'll encounter nothing but a hare, some anthills, maybe a cow. Understand?"

"Yes," he replied. "Like on a desert island."

"Right."

"Why—" he began, then broke off suddenly, scared by a host of thoughts.

"Why what?" she asked.

"Oh, nothing."

He looked at the water. He saw the shadows of the reeds at its edge. He could see two large patches, black and devoid of silver husks of light. Those were their shadows, his and the girl's.

Like on a desert island, he thought. Why like on an island? Why is it that on a desert island nudity is possible, while among other people the same nudity seems immodest and bad? I mean, a person knows everything about their own body. Everyone knows about their own stomach, chest, buttocks, thighs.... Why are those things embarrassing in the eyes of others, if everyone is somehow like one another, and so everyone knows one another? Adam and Eve went about naked in paradise, and they felt no shame. It was only when they committed a sin, by picking the fruit of the tree of knowledge of good and evil, that they were ashamed at the sight of their nakedness ...

The shadows danced on the water; the girl smiled a little mockingly, a little flirtatiously, and he saw her white teeth between her lips.

Come on now, he said to himself. Was that really how it was? Was it that particular sin which the Lord God had in mind? Adam and Eve were disobedient. To be disobedient you have to make a choice. Since they made a choice, through that they became human. Does a dog choose? Does grass choose? Even if they do, it happens without awareness ...

"Lord," said the boy all at once, for fear seized at his throat and he could no longer see the lake, or Monika, or even the sky overhead, but only the bottomless abyss of a mystery in the depths of which, far away, flickered a tiny spark of light. Lord, since they made a choice at that time, that means you ordered them quite simply to become human. . . . And it was only then they realized that they existed, that they were alive, and that they had bodies and souls. And it was then they discovered for the first time that Adam was Adam and Eve was Eve. And they saw they were different. . . . What were they ashamed of then? Themselves? That's not possible! At that time they were on a desert island. Paradise was even more than a desert island. In the entire world there were only the two of them, Adam and Eve. And yet they were ashamed. . . . What were they ashamed of?

"Monika," said the boy quietly.

She looked at him. Her eyes were full of light.

"What were Adam and Eve ashamed of in paradise?" the boy asked.

She furrowed her brow.

"What made you think of that?"

"What do you reckon? It's important. What were they ashamed of? Themselves?"

For a moment she was silent. Her expression changed; a shadow of concentration and concern settled on her forehead.

"I never thought about it," she said. "But I guess so."

"Yes? They were ashamed of themselves?" the boy repeated with deliberation. "All that time they had gone about naked without a care in the world; then all of a sudden they started to be ashamed . . ."

"She picked the apple," said the girl. "The serpent tempted her."

"The serpent doesn't matter," said the boy. "She matters. She gave in to his persuasions. She had free choice. She could have walked away from the tree."

"And what then?" asked Monika.

They looked intently at one other.

"That's the point," said the boy. "But she didn't walk away. She picked the apple and gave it to Adam to eat. In that way they both chose."

"I don't get it. Chose what? The apple?"

"Oh, Monika!" he exclaimed. "You're so . . . such a real woman."

She gave a delighted laugh.

"That's good. But why?"

"Because you only pay attention to details. I'm concerned with something greater . . . "

"What?"

He wasn't able to answer. She'd made him lose his train of thought with that apple. Everything had become muddled up for him at virtually the last moment.

A woman, he thought. A dame. Woman. Dame.

He felt a strange sadness. He sat without moving. He looked at the water. Something had escaped him. He knew it was terribly important, maybe even more important than the nakedness and shame that had given him cause for reflection. Once again in the depths of his heart he repeated the same curious question: What were they ashamed of?

* * *

They entered a shady vista between the alders. It was close; a storm was brewing. The sky to the south had clouded over, and a hot wind had blown up, bending the tops of the trees. Monika was ahead, with the boy behind her. He tore off a small alder leaf, put it between his teeth, and bit into it. He felt a bitter taste in his mouth.

"The leaves are bitter," he said.

"Then don't eat them. You're not a goat," she retorted.

"I'm not eating them. I just tried one. I'd never bitten into a leaf before."

The wind whistled through the treetops. The boy looked up and saw the arched branches. His gaze dropped down the trunk of an alder to the path. Grasses, herbs, nettles, and pink flowers in the undergrowth. And on the sand, her footprints. She was barefoot. Her feet were small, slim, and suntanned. Her footprints were shallow and faint, because she was light. He looked at her footprints. Then at her shapely tanned feet moving rhythmically. He could see her calves. A little higher up was the outline of her thighs and buttocks, her clinging dress stuck to them.

The wind hit the treetops and ran noisily across the branches.

"Hurry up," said Monika. "There's going to be a storm."

"So what?" he said.

His voice sounded almost angry. She paused for a moment. She turned round. They looked each other in the eye. She continued on. Now her footprints were somewhat deeper, her pace quicker. She broke into a run.

"Monika!" called the boy.

"There's a storm coming!" she shouted and rushed off ahead.

He ran too. He could see the girl's feet flashing, her pink soles, the cloth of her dress rippling over her buttocks. He felt the pounding of his heart. The wind whipped his face. It crossed his mind that she had taken fright. He was going to shout and ask what she was afraid of, but at that moment she burst out laughing. They ran out of the alder grove into open ground. In front of them, in the rust-colored brilliance of the sun breaking through the clouds, the manor buildings could be seen. The white columns of the veranda, the gray wall around the lawn, the blackened sides of the barns, the yellow and blue beehives in the orchard.

On the veranda stood Pilecki, looking in their direction and shading his eyes with his hand.

Everything suddenly went dark in the playroom. It happened almost in a single moment. The entire room was plunged in a murky suspension that seeped in through the windows. The daylight vanished somewhere; even the ruddy glow of the sun was swept away by the first impact of the rainstorm.

The boy stood in the middle of the room, entranced. Never before had he seen nature so elemental. In town everything took place gently, as if the natural world stopped at the city gates, frightened and embarrassed. Among the walls of the apartment buildings, in the light of street lamps, under the impermeable roofs, in the ordered reality of the immobile furniture, unfeeling lightbulbs, sturdy drains and guttering in steel mounts, the wind and the rainstorm seemed tame. The rain rattled on roofs and windowpanes, the wind here and there lashed the branches of the few trees, while streams of frothing water, brought under control, flowed down into the gutters; and humans watched this display from their dry, watertight apartments, as from a box in the theater.

Here darkness fell abruptly, as though someone had thrown an impenetrable cloak over the world. For a moment the sky turned dirty gray, as if thickened with cream; then it was extinguished in a uniform dark blue. The rainstorm struck. It was not that there were the first drops, ever bigger and more frequent; instead, at once there poured down streams of water, swollen, raging torrents. It was a wall of rain, but without the silvery beauty and pliancy that the boy was accustomed to during storms in Warsaw. The floods of water washed out the whole landscape; it was impossible to make out the columns of the veranda, the trunks of trees, or the wall around the lawn.

This was accompanied by a fearsome clatter, as if someone were flailing the roof and the walls. Pilecki didn't manage to close the door of the veranda in time, and in an instant the foaming streams of water gushed into the room, spattering the furniture. The wind passed over the house once and twice, as if in warning, then crashed against the windows with a ferocious force. It dragged a broken hornbeam branch along the veranda, threw it against the wall of the house, then snatched it up again. The sound of breaking glass rang out. An upstairs window had smashed like a soap bubble.

A swift-flowing torrent rushed down the steps of the veranda, carrying with it upturned wicker chairs, a small table, baskets and flowerpots. The poplars on the avenue in the park, always so slim and upright, were bent into monstrous humps; something in them was cracking noisily, and this was the only dry sound in this madness of watery explosions, rumbles, crashes, lashings, smacks, and whistlings.

The wind quieted down suddenly for a moment; it was clearly gathering strength, for it threw itself at the house again, battering the windowpanes, roof, and walls with streams of water. In the air, above the earth, a solid sheet of rain began to spin and broke up into hundreds of cracking whips, with which the gale buffeted the terrified manor.

Pilecki lit a cigarette; the glow of the match illuminated the playroom, summoning Monika's face from the darkness. She was sitting at the other end of the room, her elbow resting on an escritoire, staring at the boy. In the sultry, close air of the room their eyes met for a moment and hurriedly parted, as if scalded. . . . Pilecki extinguished the match. Now the tip of his cigarette could be seen; it zigzagged upward toward his mouth, where it stopped moving. Pilecki said very quietly:

"Monika, I don't like you staying out so long . . ."

The boy stiffened, waiting for her voice. He heard a faint sigh, nothing more. Then Pilecki again:

"Where were you?"

"At the lake."

Her voice floated across from far away, as though from the far bank of a river.

"Yes," said Pilecki meaninglessly. Again the gleaming pink tip of the cigarette shook and plunged downward. It danced there loosely for a moment, then before long climbed back up its gentle incline to Pilecki's mouth.

The world outside was roaring; the savage waters were drowning untold hordes of insects and millions of herbs, grasses, and flowers that exuberated upon the earth; the furious winds were tearing leaves from the trees, breaking branches, and up-rooting young oak and alder saplings and acacia bushes. White-crested waves churned up the lake, while the dirty foam washed up fragments of stalks from the slimy depths.

A peal of thunder rang out, and with it the whole play-room was lit up by a flash of lightning. A thunderbolt struck an old hornbeam in the park; a blue and white streak of light shot down from the top of the tree to its trunk.

Someone shouted at the other end of the house.

And again, from slightly farther off, there came a light-ning flash from the black, virtually invisible wall of trees in the park. Thunder rolled across the lawn, brushing against the roof of the house till the furniture in the room trembled. And again came a cry from somewhere, watery, flat, as if it were rising up from the depths.

The glow of the cigarette fell limply down, came to a stop, and gradually began going out. Pilecki said:

"I won't allow that."

"I don't understand," said the girl, from far off.

"You will," said Pilecki, somehow weakly and without conviction.

"It's stifling in here," said the boy.

"It is," agreed Pilecki.

Suddenly, in the darkness and the tumult of the world, a yellow light appeared. It crept toward the playroom from the other end of the house, moving steadily across the floor and the walls.

At the threshold of the room stood Miss Cecylia with a kerosene lamp in her hand.

"What a beautiful thunderstorm," she chirped in her bird-like voice. "I can't remember one like this for ages. . . . It's striking close to us!"

She said this the way seasoned soldiers speak of an artillery bombardment.

"It hit the hornbeams," said Pilecki concernedly. "The hornbeams always get it. Probably because I care about them the most."

"You are funny," said the old lady. "Lightning doesn't choose which source of sawmill wood to hit."

"Leave off!" said Pilecki.

At this second another flash of lightning burst into the room, followed by a peal of thunder. The windowpanes rattled, and the tiny flame of the lamp in Miss Cecylia's hands wavered and rose upward in a yellow streak.

"That was in the fields," said the old lady.

Pilecki nodded. Then he said:

"Monika was at the lake. For three hours . . . "

"Three hours," repeated Miss Cecylia. "At the lake . . . It's nice there, isn't it? It's ever so long since I've been that far. But I'll take myself there, I will. . . . I need more exercise."

Once again the room lit up and a rumbling passed over the house.

"It's moving toward Niemirów," said Monika. "There'll probably be a fire in town."

"Maybe," murmured Pilecki. "What time is it?"

He went over to the clock that stood in the corner of the room. He lifted his head and peered through the gloom at the hands.

"It's four already," he said. "Soon it'll be teatime."

The storm was growing quieter in the distance. The rain dripped down lazily, having lost its vehemence. The patter of raindrops on the windows could be heard. Water roared along the gutter on the veranda. Dull-colored torrents raced across the earth, along the wall around the lawn. Things grew a little brighter; the sky could be seen again, gray, dense as mud. The corner of the barn bared its roof trusses where a part of the thatch had been blown off. On the other side of the courtyard an uprooted acacia bush was floating by on a fast-moving current of water. A covering of fallen leaves was sweeping the veranda and the walls of the house. The wind was still bending the trees, furiously shaking their tops, but it no longer had the strength to break them.

Heavy footsteps sounded on the stairs. Pilecki said quietly, composing his words with an effort:

"Did you hear, Aunt Cylka? I said that Monika spent three hours at the lake. What do you say to that?"

"Just so," answered the old lady. "I say that Monika is a very good child."

Major Kurtz entered the playroom. He was wearing canvas shorts and a thin shirt. In the light of the lamp his face shone moistly, as if he were coming back from outside and had been soaked in the rain.

"It's terribly close," said Kurtz. "Couldn't we open a window?"

"We'd get drenched!" said Pilecki.

"Oh, right," agreed Kurtz. A trickle of perspiration ran down his forehead and along the base of his nose toward his mouth. He sat down heavily on the sofa, near the clock.

"Begging your pardon, ma'am," he murmured in the old lady's direction. "I feel dreadful."

At this moment the rain stopped abruptly; there could be heard only the splash of isolated drops and the gush of flowing water. The wind was soughing more gently, and the tops of the poplars were slowly straightening up. Pilecki strode energetically to the window and lifted the latch. He pushed the pane. A stream of bitter, slippery cold entered the room. Kurtz stood, went up to the door, opened it wide, and walked out onto the veranda. He took a deep breath. A darkish streamlet of sweat was drying on the nape of his neck.

"It's lovely!" called the major.

Pilecki went back to the other end of the room.

"You can put the lamp out now, Aunt Cylka. It's not needed anymore," he said.

The old lady obediently turned down the wick and blew out the little flame. Then Pilecki said a few words to her in a muffled, fierce voice. She raised her eyes and looked at him like a sick bird. With sadness, resignation, and aversion.

The boy heard Pilecki's voice saying:

"You must understand that, Aunt Cylka."

And the voice of the old lady replying:

"Yes. And what of it, tell me that?"

Major Kurtz ran from the veranda onto the driveway, leaping over the foaming streams of water. He was neighing harshly like a horse. But that was just his laugh . . .

After the storm had passed, the boy wanted to go for a walk with Monika. But she was nowhere to be found. He searched for her throughout the deserted house, but in vain. He climbed the stairs to the attic where Pilecki lived and knocked at his host's door. No one was in. So he returned downstairs, sat on the sofa in the playroom, and waited idly.

Close by he heard footsteps along with the clatter of crockery and the rustle of a tablecloth. It was Mania, their maid from Warsaw, and the local cook laying the table for tea.

Sunshine cleansed by the thunderstorm poured into the room. Everything in the world gleamed cleanly; raindrops glittered on the branches of acacias and lilacs, the air was fresh, and the heat had abated. Somewhere a dog was barking; the ringing of metal against metal could be heard. It was a farmhand sharpening a scythe behind the barns.

He went back upstairs, prowled the entire house, and was amazed to realize that he had been left completely on his own. Everyone had disappeared. His parents' room smelled of eau de cologne; there was a coating of powder on the commode beneath the mirror, the wardrobe was open, and an unfinished glass of milk stood on the windowsill. He had the unpleasant impression that his parents had left the room in a hurry.

He returned to the playroom with a heavy step, went out onto the veranda, sat in a damp armchair, and closed his eyes. He had a sense of unutterable loneliness. He suddenly realized that he was more apart than he had ever been, that everything about was alien and no longer belonged to him. He opened his eyes and looked at the drying courtyard, the lawn covered with weeds, and the gate to the park, beyond which extended the road to the village. He saw the trees, the sky, the faun on its mossy plinth, and a dog running behind the barn. It was all separate and independent of him; he felt that between him and the world there had arisen a barrier which was hard to cross and which restricted him and imprisoned him in his loneliness. The passing thought, or rather presentiment, came to him that this was precisely the answer to his nagging question about what the first people in paradise had been ashamed of; but he couldn't hold onto this thought. A lazy sadness took over his mind.

A tiny ladybug landed on his hand. He closed his eyes again. Now his imagination began to work laboriously. But not like it usually did, when events, outlines of figures, and adventures passed through his head at breakneck speed, when he crossed huge distances, in a single moment leaving the North Pole to find himself in India, or quitting the battlefield for the deck of a sailing ship. Now images came to him slowly, and he had to make an effort to remove from view the successive slides of his magic lantern. And these were by no means colored visions, as once before.

He was alone on a stony road on which there were no trees, plants, or animals. Above him, the vault of the sky, in which the sun was not shining. Under his feet, gray oval-shaped boulders or pebbles, which, when he nudged them with his foot, made no sound. He heard the gentle soughing of the wind, but he knew it was the real wind passing across the lawn and the veranda. Yet where he was now there was no wind, there were no clouds, nor anything that could be regarded as a sign of life.

On this road he felt tired and devoid of hope, but he felt no fear. Indifference, rather. Where am I going? he asked himself. Where is this road leading me? On the ash-gray horizon, against a background of shapeless clouds, he saw the silhouette of a figure. He drew closer to it, or rather it floated toward him, because he himself, though he was moving, remained in one place. He recognized Christ on the cross. The figure's eyes were open wider than ever before. And the two of them stared at each other intently. This lasted a long while, and then Christ's eyelids closed, and His body, spread-eagled on the cross, slumped somehow powerlessly and stopped moving. Now He has died, the boy thought.

He felt no fear or pain; he was indifferent. Once again, from somewhere in the house, he could hear the sounds of voices, the slap of bare feet on the tiled floor, and the rattle of plates.

Lord God, he said to Christ on the cross, why do You have to die? Is it to set me an example and to persuade me to resign myself to what awaits me too?

He set off again down the stony road, and again the rocks he kicked moved away soundlessly from beneath his feet. He was alone; Christ had vanished in the grayness of the horizon. Then he felt a painful weight in his heart. What a pity, he thought. What a pity. . . . For a moment he was choked by despair.

He felt someone touch his arm, and he turned his head. Against the gray sky stood his mother. Her hand strayed to his hair and passed through it. He knew that this was a loving caress, but he could not feel her touch. His mother's face was good, beautiful, indistinct. She said something; he saw her lips moving, but did not hear the words. It was agonizing.

Once more he stood alone on the road, among the rocks, and the ashen sky hung over his head. His father's face floated toward him, then the faces of his grandmother, his teachers, and his classmates. There came toward him bizarre shapes that he had difficulty recognizing, and laboriously reconstructed. These were games and pastimes he had abandoned long ago, lead soldiers, balls and bows, toy ships and revolvers, and also children's clothes, books, notebooks, pencils, lengths of string he had played with, metal buttons and lumps of plasticine, bead abacuses, teddy bears, Eliza the pony and the table in the park café he had once frequented with his grandmother, the postcards from his grandmother's dresser, her embroidery and porcelain, the portrait of Aunt Magdalena in her crimson dress and wide hat, and that age-blackened picture showing a boat on a stormy sea.

All this whirled around noiselessly on the gray horizon, which disappeared from view in the throng of people, objects, blurred forms and flashes of unthinking premonitions. And this vortex was slowly collapsing and losing its shape, as if a rainstorm were washing away each barely apprehended image.

And again he was alone. But now he had before him darkness instead of the gray, stony road. And through this darkness a stream of sunlight broke through his eyelids. He opened his eyes. He stirred. The ladybug flew from his hand. In the dining room at the other end of the house bare feet were pattering once again.

He thought to himself that it had been a dream that had lasted a mere second. He looked ahead soberly. He saw the lawn, the park, the barns, the road, the dog. He heard the whetstone tapping against the scythe.

He stood up and went into the playroom, then along the hallway to the stairs and up the stairs to the second floor. He opened the door to his room. He lay on his bed like that time, years before, in the cabin on the river boat.

So I am, he thought. So I quite simply am!

And he decided that before the day was out he would kiss Monika on the lips.

A mild evening set in; elongated shadows lay across the ground, and the sky retained a red glow. Crickets began to chirp, while the birds fell silent. The air was cool; reflections of light slid across its smooth surface.

After supper the company went for a walk. Even Miss Cecilia decided to take a stroll, despite Miss Róża's words of warning.

And so everyone went, all in one big group, around the lawn and then down the avenue to the gate. The boy's father and Major Kurtz were in front, and in between them the boy's mother, to whom they both lent their arm. A few paces behind, Aunt Cecylia tottered along, supported by Pilecki; then came Monika and the boy. Malinowski, the steward, after he had circled the lawn, scuttled away and vanished in the shadow of the barns.

Things were not so harmonious as they appeared, however. Miss Cecylia, always hungry for conversation, kept pulling Pilecki toward the trio in the lead, while he was reluctant to yield to the old lady's urgings and dawdled in the rear.

"Come on, now," his aunt grumbled. "Aren't you the slow-poke!"

"What's the hurry," Pilecki would say each time.

Since he was stronger and was holding her by the arm, Miss Cecylia at times squirmed like a squirrel caught in a net.

At the gate the major's orderly stood smoking a cigarette. He threw it to the ground, crushed it with his foot, and straightened up, clicking his heels.

"How are things, Piotrowski?" asked the major.

"The air's pleasant, sir," replied the soldier.

The company passed the orderly and walked out onto the road that led to the village. The boy turned round and looked once again at the soldier. Out of the corner of his eye he spotted the shadow of another figure among the trees. He gave a laugh.

"What's so funny?" asked Monika.

"Our Mania's out for a walk too," he murmured.

"Good for her," said Monika.

"What? What were you saying?" put in Pilecki. He stopped for a moment, in spite of Miss Cecylia's objections.

"Nothing," replied Monika.

"I don't like walking like this," croaked Miss Cecylia. "We're not at a funeral here . . . "

She freed her arm and moved away. Pilecki followed her. He wore an angry expression.

"Monika," whispered the boy, "what is it that he wants from you?"

"It's funny," she answered. "He's looking after me."

Suddenly he shivered, as he felt a delicate touch on his forearm. She brushed it with her fingertips and at once withdrew her hand. They looked into each other's eyes.

Why is it so light, he thought. He was beginning to feel angry at the sun for setting so sluggishly. All at once everything seemed distinct, outlined in sharp contours.

Pilecki had moved further away; his green jacket blended into the background of the trees.

"What are you going to do after you graduate from high school?" said the boy. His voice sounded wooden.

"I don't know," she replied. "I still have time to think about it."

"I'm going to study law," he said, surprised himself at this thought, which had entered his head for the first time. He immediately addressed the next thought: Why law? Where had this stupid idea come from? And at once he reconciled himself to law. He saw himself in judge's robes, at a table over which hung the White Eagle, emblem of the republic. He thought to himself that this wasn't so bad . . .

"That's right," he said with a certain satisfaction. "I chose the law because it's difficult and responsible work."

"You'll be like Woźnicki," said Monika.

"Woźnicki?"

"The attorney from Niemirów. He manages some business for my uncle. Sometimes he visits us and then the two of them sit in the playroom or on the veranda and shout at each other."

"They argue?" asked the boy.

"No. Woźnicki's a bit deaf."

"Lawyers aren't always attorneys. I may become a judge or a public prosecutor."

"Come off it."

She pulled off a sprig of acacia and began stripping off the leaves.

"Are you telling your fortune?" he asked.

She looked him in the eyes and smiled.

"I don't need to," she replied. "The future doesn't interest me."

Pilecki slowed down again and Miss Cecylia berated him.

He began to light a cigarette. He turned his head and looked straight into the boy's eyes.

"So then, Krzysztof! How do you like my place?"

It was the first time he had addressed the boy directly. His voice was oddly resonant, his gaze penetrating.

"It's wonderful," replied the boy. "This is a real vacation."

"It's a wilderness here," said Pilecki. "Woods, water. And regular people. That's the most important thing. We had a splendid storm, didn't we?"

"Yes," said the boy. "I'd never seen anything like it."

"That was nothing," interrupted Pilecki. "I remember a storm that brought down several hundred trees round the lake. When was that, eh? What do you think, Aunt Cylka?"

Miss Cecylia raised her tiny eyes and stared at Pilecki.

"A long time back," she replied. "Years ago . . . "

He nodded, drew on the cigarette, and blew smoke right into the boy's face. The four of them stood together in the filtered pink light of the sunset. All about them was the smell of mowed hay, acacia, and unhappiness.

"Tomorrow," said Pilecki, "I'm driving to Niemirów. You'll go with me, Monika."

"All right," she answered.

"You were talking about Woźnicki, eh? That's who I have to see. He likes you. So does Mrs. Woźnicka. We'll stay for lunch with them."

Monika nodded. The boy felt a pulsing in his temples. Pilecki blew out smoke once again. The boy's mother and father and the major had disappeared round a curve in the road.

"It's getting cool," said Aunt Cecylia. "We should be heading back."

"Yes," said Pilecki. "You'll catch a chill, Aunt. Take your grandmother back to the house."

"Oh, that's not necessary," protested the old lady.

"Out of the question," said Pilecki.

Monika gave Miss Cecylia her arm. They turned back toward the gates.

"Let's take a stroll, eh?" Pilecki murmured to the boy.

The boy nodded. They moved off. The crickets were singing desperately. Over the treetops a sudden clatter was heard, and the dark shape of a hawk soared upward.

"He's spotted something," said Pilecki.

"What?"

"Maybe a hare . . . "

The hawk gave up and drifted slowly away into the darkness, toward the trees around the lake.

"It's beautiful here, isn't it?" said Pilecki. "A great empty world. For you it's something new. In Warsaw there are so many people, it's seething with life. Here things are different."

"I don't like crowds," said the boy. "This is good."

Pilecki threw down the cigarette and crushed it with his heel, as the orderly by the gate had. All at once he gave a deep sigh and passed his palm across his face as if he wanted to wipe off the sweat.

"It's a great pity that war is coming," he said softly.

"I don't think there'll be war, Captain," said the boy.

"There will, for sure there will. And then we'll go to fight. You too! How old are you actually?"

"I just turned fifteen."

"You're a real man. Do you know that for three years I never left the trenches?"

"I heard. My father told me."

"Right. And now war's coming again."

He said this in a strange way; he was morose, but was not particularly resentful or concerned. It was as if he were far from bothered by the idea of leaving this countryside and returning to the trenches. He said sourly:

"Soon we'll go to this new war. And we'll lose!"

"Why would we lose?" objected the boy.

"Because we're weaker. And the weaker side always loses. However much they want to win, they always lose."

They reached the bend in the road and saw the outlines of the other three in the distance, in the gathering gloom.

"The Germans have tanks and artillery. They have planes. In Spain they bombed towns, villages, farmland. We'll lose the war."

"Don't talk like that, Captain!" the boy said. "You never can tell . . ."

"That depends. Some can tell, others can't," said Pilecki tartly. "For example, I can tell only too well."

"How?"

Pilecki tapped his forehead with his index finger.

"I think, that's all," he said.

They were walking slowly; underfoot they could feel the earth wet from the storm.

"Do you have many friends?" asked Pilecki.

The boy hesitated. Not because he wanted to give an exact answer, but because he was struck by Pilecki's voice. There was a new note in it, a sharp and disquieting tone.

"There are twenty-three boys in my class," he replied. "But that doesn't mean anything."

"I understand," said Pilecki quietly. "I only had one true friend in school. He's no longer alive. My other classmates I can hardly remember."

Once again he stopped for a moment and took his packet of cigarettes from the pocket of his jacket.

"Do you smoke?" he asked.

"No," the boy lied.

"I don't believe you. When I was your age I was smoking—in secret, of course."

"Exactly," said the boy.

"You can have one. I won't tell your father," said Pilecki.

"That's not what it's about," said the boy. "I'm not afraid of my father."

"Well then?"

He offered him the open packet.

"No, thank you," said the boy. "Maybe another time."

"As you wish," murmured Pilecki, and lit a cigarette himself. In the flare of the match the boy saw his wrinkled face and drooping eyelids. It was an evil face; some bad deed was written in it. Pilecki threw the match into the grass.

"And what about girls?" he said.

"I don't understand."

"You understand perfectly. You're almost an adult. How do you stand as far as those things are concerned?"

"Captain," murmured the boy, embarrassed.

"All right, all right," said Pilecki in an angry voice. "Never mind."

All of a sudden he called loudly into the depths of the darkness, where the shadows moving away from them could barely be seen.

"Seweryn! Time to go back. It's night!"

"True!" shouted back the boy's father. "We'll be right with you!"

Pilecki turned back toward the manor without a word. They walked in silence. The boy was seized by anxiety mixed with anger. What does he want from me? he thought worriedly. When they entered the avenue, Pilecki said:

"I'm glad you all came to stay with me. The old ladies have perked up. Me too."

In order to appear sociable and well-mannered, and also in the hope that the unpleasant impression from the walk would pass, the boy said:

"Yes. It's beautiful here. And the manor's so old. It must be over a hundred years old."

"Over a hundred," agreed Pilecki.

"I expect it was one of your ancestors who built it, is that right, Captain?"

"I couldn't say. . . . Someone built it, someone let it get run-down, someone else will finish off the job."

In one of the windows of the house the glow of a lamp could be seen. She lit a lamp, the boy thought to himself. So I wouldn't get lost.

But when they went into the manor, it turned out the lamp was standing in the playroom, and in its yellow circle Miss Cecylia was playing solitaire.

And so when he went to bed he was furious. He felt like scratching the wall with his fingernails. The girl had gotten away from him, and the whole world was against him. He could feel his back sweating. His anger was choking him; it was like a gag stuck between his teeth.

Then suddenly he felt relief. Night's falling now, he thought, and in a few hours another new day will begin. Tomorrow! Tomorrow everything I wish for will be realized . . .

He turned to the wall and half-closed his eyes. He resigned himself. For the first time in his life he resigned himself, and it amazed him. Never before had he experienced the taste of patient waiting. What was happening within him now was new and foreign, yet he understood that he still remained himself and that he had himself to thank for this new discovery. He had a sense of calm and wondered why he was so calm. After all, I lost, he thought. Everything let me down. Including her! She agreed so obediently to turn back to the house, leaving me at Pilecki's side without a single word, without even a look. . . . Why am I calm? I'm calm because nothing ends today, he answered himself with a solemnity that also surprised him. Tomorrow, in the course of the day I'll kiss her. It's decided. When I get up in the morning Monika won't be there. I won't see her. I'll wait all day till she comes back from Niemirów. In the evening, the thing I have planned will come to pass.

He arrived at the conviction that one day and one night meant nothing. The coming day is going to drag on, he thought. And immediately he added in consolation: Don't they all drag on? The hours at his school desk seemed interminable, the journey home lasted forever, dinner in the company of his parents, in the dining room flooded with sunlight, at the table covered with a damask tablecloth, melted and was washed away in time, amid the chimes of the clock striking the quarters, in the rattle of plates and cutlery, in the silence and tedium of digestion. Then came the after-dinner hours, greenish in the springtime, yellow in the fall, ash-gray in winter, hours of silence in the house in which dust from the carpets danced in the rays of the sun, the sun's rays slid across the pages of his notebooks, and stray flies drowned in the inkwell. Those hours were like cooling lava or plasticine stretched into a thin band. It was a kind of swamp that cannot be skirted but has to be crossed step by step, in boredom, exhaustion, resignation, with no hope of change, because when the dark of evening finally came, that cooling lava would solidify into a certain ritual, suppertime would arrive, back to the dining room, in the spring still brightened by the sun hunched over the rooftops, in the winter lit by a chandelier. The time for supper, and so once again Mania's quiet footsteps around the table, his mother's preserves on a little cut-glass plate, her strong tea and crumbs from her roll, his father's slices of bread and jam, eggshells, fruit knives, apple peel, cigar smoke, the murmur of voices, flat, spent words, sometimes the ringing of the telephone at the other end of the apartment and the grimace on his father's face as he stood heavily, crossed the room, and closed the door behind him, accompanied by his mother's gaze, in which curiosity and reproach could be seen. And so suppertime was a continuation of those miry depths in which time plunged the boy at the moment of his return from school. And later the evening ritual took on a different consistency. There was in it something irrevocable, inescapable, like the last minutes of a condemned prisoner. The bathroom, the plash of water, his toothbrush, the coarse towel, slippery soap, the scent of mint mixed with the faint smell of gas, warm water on his skin, then finally the cold sheets and the turning off of the light.

Until this moment he had moved with a sense of imprisonment, fettered by injunctions that were terrible perhaps not so much because they were evil but because they were unambiguous and monotonous. It was only when the light went out and he closed his eyes that there appeared within him a lively, bustling world which was constantly changing and surprising him.

Virtually all day long, from the time he woke up till the last few minutes before falling asleep, he had sensed time through the pores of his skin, through hearing and smell. This time was hard at school and soft at home; clamorous noises during lessons, even in the quiet moments in class when the boys bent over their notebooks and it seemed that only the scraping of nibs could be heard. Even then time was loud and resonant, filled with the whine of trams, the clatter of horses' hooves, the shouts of children playing on the squares, the hum of the crowds, and the whisper of the wind outside the window. It was a loud, cantankerous time, turgid as a tradeswoman haggling at market. And it had its own peculiar smell, a combination of wax, chalk, cloth, human bodies, and musty interiors.

Time at home was soft. The hours passed through the rooms, brushing against the cut-glass wineglasses and the porcelain on the dressers, tapping the top plate of the kitchen stove, sounding in the water pipes, and sometimes touching the telephone and making it ring in desperation, muffled by carpets, books, and human absence. That time too had its smell, singularly elegant: A whole bouquet of scents resided in the golden vases of the afternoon, the scent of cosmetics and cigars, roast beef and fruit, dust on the books, starched covers on the furniture in the living room, and also something intangible and mild that dominated everything else yet remained nameless.

Everything, both at school and at home, on the streets and among the schoolbooks in which he immersed himself—everything was constant and unchanging. The world remained still; thanks to this he was able to explore it, but he hadn't discovered anything worth paying attention to. Did he not know like the back of his hand the desks at school, the cupboards filled with exhibits in the biology laboratory, and the glistening map placed on the easel during geography lessons?

He knew the burned taste of milk and the nauseating taste of ersatz coffee poured into metal mugs in the long recess. He knew what to expect on the playing fields, in the gym, and in the physics laboratory.

Did he not know like the back of his hand the thirty-seven marble steps that led to the second floor of his apartment building; the pedestal on the landing, where against the pointed arch of the window there lurked the plaster figure of Fortune with a cornucopia; and the great honey-colored door that led to their apartment? When he approached it and rang the bell, he knew with absolute certainty that in a moment he would hear the swish of Mania's footsteps, the click of the lock, a creak—and that he would find himself in the gloom of the foyer, among the coatracks, umbrella stands, small wicker armchairs, and engravings of landscapes of old Warsaw. He knew he would encounter Mania's bovine gaze as she exclaimed in a flutter: "Oh

Lord! Are you back already?" and ran to the kitchen to clatter the pots and pans, always surprised in the same way that time, which for him dragged on interminably, flew past so quickly, confounding all her plans. And he would, with the weary step of an old man, walk down the hallway to the right to a closet and see that indestructible glory hole of toys removed from the child's room. Entering this room, he would sit by the window, stare at the chestnut trees, the clouds, a horse and carriage, and wait to be told that the meal was ready.

Did he not know like the back of his hand that world of which he constituted a small part and which was a small part of him? And had he not been long surprised that nothing transpired from these organic relations? That surprise was his only surprise amid the familiar, tedious days, hours, and minutes, which he urged desperately to pass more quickly. But they were stubborn; they dragged on dolefully, beginning with Mania's touch as she woke him, always a little embarrassed, saying, "Get up, Krzysiek, it's almost seven," to breakfast in the kitchen, at the table with its oilcloth cover, in the patter of feet on the thirty-seven steps, in the dust of morning, the shudder of the bus turning a half circle in front of City Hall, in the bright sunlight, the first bell, lessons, between fingers dirty with chalk, between the pages of textbooks and notebooks, on the green linoleum of the school corridors, and then across the square, across the roadway, where on cold days the horse manure was steaming, through the gate of the gardens, along the graveled path, around the fountain, through another gate, along another sidewalk, to the courtyard that formed a passageway, where in the very center of the city, amid the imposing apartment buildings, chickens wandered about and a dog barked as

Andrzej Szczypiorski

it strained at its chain, through another dark gateway, toward
the thirty-seven marble steps, to the honey-colored door, along
the hallway, past the glory hole, to the window in his room,
to the chestnut tree, the clouds, the carriage, till dinnertime,
where there was the damask tablecloth, vase, plates, roast,
mother, father, cigar, clock, dust, telephone, voices, words,
flat, worn out, indifferent, to textbooks and notebooks, a fly
in the inkpot, the scratching of the nib, the sun hunched over
the rooftops, Mania, soft-boiled eggs, fruit knives, supper,
mother, cigar, clock, father, telephone, mint, roaring gas, bare
feet on the stone floor, the banded stove resting on bear's-feet,
Mania, sheet, telephone, father, the switch of the bedside
lamp, darkness, eyelids, once again the telephone, once again
mother, once again a horse on the cobblestones, almost the
end, just another moment, I love you God, I love you Mama,
I love you Papa, I love you Berta, I love you grandmother, I
love you Krzyś, at last the South Sea islands, palms, a gentle
sea breeze, an African torso, the Congo, Hawaii, General Nobile
in his dirigible amid the Arctic ice, an attack by Indians, a
woman's breast, her lips, hot, everywhere hot, it's a sin, Christ
have mercy on me, sleep, sleep, the end of everything, the end
of everything till tomorrow!

He lay without moving. He could feel the straw of the mattress,
the linen of the sheet, and the wall that his arm was touching.
The moon was in the middle of the room. Far beyond the lake
a wild peacock called.

One day and one night, thought the boy; that doesn't count! I'll go swimming till midday, he thought, then I'll dry off in the sun. I'll wait patiently. I'll eat lunch on the veranda, and during dessert I'll say that I'm going for a walk in the woods. My father will say nothing, my mother will nod, the major will come out with something silly, and the old ladies will smile. I'll go off into the trees, then when I've disappeared from view, I'll head down the road toward Niemirów. I'll meet the wagonette. I'll sit on the bench opposite Monika. My knees will be touching hers.

He thought this, but at the same time he thought something else too. That he wouldn't go swimming and dry off, that he wouldn't eat dinner and wouldn't go out toward Niemirów to meet the two of them, and wouldn't sit on the bench and touch Monika's knee with his own. Because he would be seized with fear, overcome with anxiety in the presence of his mother, his father, the major, the old ladies, and above all Pilecki.

I'm alone, he thought bitterly, and even she is against me. When she comes back from Niemirów in the late afternoon, she won't want to look me in the eye. At supper she'll sit at a distance, then immediately after the meal she'll disappear to the other end of the house, like today during the storm. I'll search for her in the empty rooms, but everywhere I'll find only traces of an earlier presence, covered with dust, cobwebs, and disdain.

He tried to get to sleep, to escape from these unpleasant thoughts. But he was unable to drive away the images of failure. It seemed to him that he was once again to encounter the disappointments he had experienced not long ago, when he had kissed a woman for the first time.

The moon alighted on the very edge of the bed; the peacock beyond the lake had fallen silent. Outside the window
everything was quiet, dead, cold, slippery.

Oh, how stupid that kiss had been . . .

That day they had visited the tailor's. To be more precise, they
had gone to run various errands in town, and had finished at
the tailor's. On that day Mania had had a cold and had stayed
in bed, and so the boy's parents had taken with them Aunt
Magdalena's maid, whose name was Justyna. She was a tall,
rather thin young woman, with a dark-complexioned face and
a pink birthmark on her forehead. It was said that as a child she
had been in a fire and had been saved at the last minute. She
had a peculiar relationship with Aunt Magdalena; she was more
a confidante of the lady, who led a somewhat tempestuous existence, a fact which, incidentally, was frowned upon by the rest
of the family. Justyna wore Aunt Magdalena's elegant dresses,
her shoes and hats, and so she looked like a lady of the world.
She had a talent for mimicry, and observed not just her mistress's
way of life but also her gestures and expressions. She wore make-
up. She smoked cigarettes. She behaved familiarly with the men
who visited Aunt Magdalena and brought bouquets of flowers
and boxes of chocolates.

The day they went to town together so the boy's mother
could have some help with the shopping, the maid was wearing
a smart jacket, a tight skirt, and a little hat decorated with a
feather. It was April, and the afternoon was quite warm. In the

horse-drawn cab the boy's parents sat on the seat, and Justyna and the boy on the fold-down bench. Justyna said that the colonel had gained weight.

"Our colonel's put on a lot of weight, ma'am," she said.

"Miss Justyna!" whispered the boy's mother, pursing her lips. His father looked away, at the sidewalk, as if he had no desire whatsoever to hear or notice anything. He probably felt embarrassed by the presence of this young person, unconstrained and sure of herself, who moved in a world that he despised. The boy's father could not tolerate Aunt Magdalena precisely because she led a lifestyle that was so far removed from his own ideals. As for the colonel, he was a friend of Aunt Magdalena's, a tenacious suitor who for years had never given up hope. It was he who had put on weight, which meant that he had ruined his chances.

Justyna laughed. On one side she had a badly filled tooth, and so when she laughed she twisted her mouth unnaturally.

They rode around town for a long time; dusk was falling, the cab rocked from one store to the next, and at last they went to the tailor's.

The sun was setting in bluish wisps of smoke when they found themselves on a crowded Jewish street filled with carriages, pedestrians, and noise. They pulled up in front of an old apartment building; the cabdriver was told to wait. As they were entering the gate, the driver hopped down from his seat, took out a sack of oats, and gave it to the mare.

In the gateway children were playing, and a bearded Jew sat on a folding chair, eating seeds and spitting out the husks in front of him. They climbed up to the second floor, where the tailor's workshop was located. The head of the firm was waiting at the threshold, bowing. The apartment smelled of oil, onion, and figs.

"I have the feeling," said the tailor, "that you're after a new look, Doctor."

"We shall see," said the boy's father.

When they entered, a skinny journeyman with reddish hair showed the boy's mother to an armchair. She sat down and began taking off her gloves. She asked to be shown some fashion journals. The tailor, whose name was Mitelman, called loudly:

"Mr. Glas, journals for the lady."

From the other end of the apartment appeared Mr. Glas, short, fat, balding, without a jacket but wearing a vest and a felt hat, with a tape measure draped around his neck and a pincushion at his breast. He brought the latest fashion magazines from Vienna and London. The boy's mother looked through them patiently.

His father said:

"What do you have that's new, Mr. Mitelman?"

"Everything," replied Mitelman. "Everything's new. My head's spinning, it's all so new . . . "

And he led the boy's father to the wall and drew aside a blue curtain, revealing shelves of cloths. His mother looked up from her magazine.

"We're thinking about a suit for the summer," she said.

"Who would think any differently these days?" said Mitelman and added, turning to Mr. Glas: "Mr. Glas, that cheviot from Bielsko comes to mind."

"So it should," said Glas.

He took a ladder from the corner of the room, leaned it against the shelves, climbed up, and from high above he took a bolt of light blue material.

"This is a cheviot for you, Doctor," said Mitelman. "Bielsko cheviot, it speaks for itself."

"I should say," added Glas, puffing out his lips.

The boy's mother rose from the armchair and went up to the long counter on which Mitelman, with a movement that was easy and ever so slightly offhand, and yet at the same time so intensely careful, spread out the roll of cloth. Glas seized hold of the material in his hand and clenched it in his fist; his lips narrowed, his eyes too, his diaphragm rose under his vest, for he was using all his strength to try and grind the material into dust. Then he opened his hand, almost with abhorrence threw the material down on the counter, looked at the boy's father, and at his mother, and at Mitelman, and smiled triumphantly.

"Well then? How about that?" he said. "Do you see that, ma'am?"

The boy's mother said:

"Yes. But it's too light, Seweryn."

His father nodded.

"It's too light, Mr. Glas," said Mitelman. "This is no good for the doctor's blond coloring."

"What are we talking about here?" asked Glas, pushing aside the roll of cloth in disgust and clambering back up the ladder.

In the meantime Justyna had come up to the window where the boy stood. From the second floor he was watching the traffic on the street, a tram squeezing through the crowd of pedestrians on the roadway, a furniture cart trying to drive into the gateway opposite, the storekeepers on the sidewalks.

"Funny, isn't it?" said Justyna quietly.

He nodded. She rested her hand on his shoulder. She leaned forward in order to see the street more clearly.

"Goodness, how strong you are," she said even more quietly. "What big shoulders you have!"

"Sure," he answered. "What did you think, Miss?"

"Don't call me Miss, call me Justyna."

"Why?" he murmured.

"Because I feel like it."

At this moment Mr. Glas said from the other end of the room:

"That's not for you, Doctor, I swear by my own health."

"Mr. Glas," put in Mitelman, "your health is of no interest to me. But you took the words right out of my mouth."

"Nonsense," said the boy's mother. "What if it is thin? It should be thin."

"I'll show you a thin cheviot, ma'am. This isn't cheviot; this is nothing but rags!"

The boy laughed. Justyna whispered to him:

"When you laugh, your mouth looks lovely."

"And when I don't laugh?" he asked arrogantly.

"It looks lovely then too."

He began to feel a little hot. The buzz from outside the window, the sun setting over the rooftops, at the other end of the room the cheviot, Glas, Mitelman, his parents. Hot. Sticky. Lustful.

His father said:

"I think we may need the tape measure. I've put on a little weight recently . . . "

"Mr. Glas, did you hear that?" exclaimed Mitelman.

"I don't hear things like that," retorted Glas. "That's a nasty little joke. But I do mean to take the gentleman's measurements."

"This way, then, please," said Mitelman, rubbing his hands as if he had grown cold. They went through into the other room; the boy's mother returned to her armchair and her magazines. But then Mitelman exclaimed in despair:

"What am I thinking of! I have something to show you, ma'am."

He broke off and invited the boy's mother into the next room, where he stored his materials. They left. The thin reddish journeyman remained in the workshop, leaning over an ironing board. He placed a wet cloth over the material and pressed down with the iron. There was a hiss and a cloud of steam.

Mr. Glas called to the journeyman from the other room:

"Benio, bring me a lead pencil right away!"

The journeyman set the iron aside, muttered something, and went out of the shop. The sun was smoking over the roofs, a tram was ringing its bell, the vendors were shouting, the Percheron horse pulling the furniture cart dropped its head as it strained from the effort and pulled stubbornly, someone said, "You call that a lead pencil?," the boy gave a deep sigh, on his lips he felt something moist, warm, soft, a living being was penetrating his mouth, he was weak, terribly weak and at the same time in turmoil, his neck stiffened, his thighs and shoulders, his stomach and his wrists, everything in him was crying out desperately and blissfully, he felt pain and joy, it seemed to him he was dying, but he knew that he wasn't dying, he was beginning to live, only now was he beginning, after so many years of wait-ing, so many years of uncertainty, only now was he beginning to live, he was no longer grass, moss, water, he was separate and unique, he was tough and separate, he was alone and tough, he was his own person and alone, here was mouth, lips, tongue, teeth, she and he, two joined together, yet two, she was his, he was hers, they permeated each other, they created a unity, yet they were separate, she and he, the sun slipping across the roof-tops, the tram ringing, vendors shouting, the horse drawing the cart, the iron hissing on the damp cloth, Justyna's lips pulling back, her eyes mocking and brazen, Justyna whispered, "You sweet rogue!," he bent forward, searching her lips, but they were pulling back, twisted in a smile, her tongue passed across them, they were moist and glistening—and suddenly the rotten tooth was exposed, a dark, rusty mark, something old and unsightly, something alien and separate, "You sweet rogue," repeated Justyna, but this time her voice sounded low and hoarse, it had no charm, something violent was happening outside the win-dow and in the boy's heart, the horse was pulling the furniture cart onto the high curb of the sidewalk, the leather harness was stretched to its absolute limit, a vendor was tugging the sleeve of a passerby, the gaze of a policeman in his dark blue uniform, the peak of his cap reflecting the pink light of the sun, the tram stopped, Mr. Glas repeated in an angry voice, "You call this a lead pencil, you nitwit!," a child's shout rang out; and the boy felt rage, he felt like striking Justyna in the face, summoning a cry of pain from her throat, then in a single movement knock-ing her down onto the dirty floor of the shop, among the man-nequins on which jackets were tacked, knocking this girl into the dust, the grime, the pins scattered about, the ends of thread and scraps of cloth, so that her skirt rose up, baring her knees and thighs, her stockings fastened to garters, and even higher, deeper, further . . .

Mr. Glas came in, took a pencil lying on the counter, smiled apologetically, and said:

"There you are, a simple thing like a pencil . . . "

And he left the shop.

The boy wiped the sweat from his forehead. He was slowly calming down. Justyna was smiling. The furniture cart had disappeared into the gateway. The policeman had moved off; in the crowd on the sidewalk, he looked like a hundred-gun frigate among fishing skiffs. The boy's mother came in, saying:

"It's a tiny bit *altmodisch*, Mr. Mitelman."

"I'm not saying it isn't, ma'am. But *altmodisch* has its own charm . . . "

Everything cooled down. Tomorrow I'll go and visit Aunt Magdalena, the boy was thinking. I'll push Justyna into that little room by the bathroom. I'll give her something to remember me by!

Justyna looked out the window and licked her lips. It's disgusting, the boy was thinking; it's revolting. I'll push her into that room, knock her down on the bed, then she'll take her dress off. . . . No, she'll do that first, then lie down. What will I do if she doesn't want to? Come off it! She's so disgusting she's bound to want to . . .

The journeyman once again pressed the iron down on the damp cloth and once again there was a burst of steam. The boy's father appeared, followed by Mr. Glas. Then down the stairs, through the gateway, to the cab. The old Jew was sitting on his chair and spitting out the husks of seeds. Snot-nosed children grabbed hold of the wheels. They rode off. The boy's parents on the seat, Justyna and the boy on the folding bench. He could feel the warmth of Justyna's thigh. As if by mistake, he put his hand on her leg above the knee, and withdrew it at once. She didn't budge. His mother said:

"Actually, the evenings are still cool."

His father said:

"Yes; they're cool."

"But they're lovely," said Justyna.

The boy felt bitterness and disappointment. He had kissed a woman. What of it? The world hadn't changed. Neither had he.

As he was falling asleep, the wild peacock cried again far off, on the other side of the lake. The moon left the room and clung to the gutter; it hung there, quiet and helpless, tangled up in the grapevine.

I love you, Mama. I love you, Papa. I love you, Berta. I love you, grandmother. I love you, Monika.

That was his last thought.

Everything went differently from what he had anticipated. It wasn't the first time he had experienced a surprise of that kind. Perhaps for this reason, he never attached any importance to his own plans and never worried about carrying them out; he was interested in the pure exercise of the imagination. He knew that fate played tricks, and he submitted himself to this cheerfully.

And so everything went differently. The day was cloudy to begin with, the sky hanging low; at breakfast a wind blew up, bringing an irksome rain. It drizzled till lunchtime, then brightened up, but the whole day was cold. So he didn't go down to the lake. To begin with he sat on the veranda, undecided what he ought to do, and enlivened by the hope that in a quarter of an hour the weather would clear up. Then he gave up, took a few books from Pilecki's library, and wandered up to his room. In this way he was saved. At first he approached the books mistrustfully, just as a way to kill time. Yet his thoughts quickly fell into their trap. He was captivated by Flaubert.

The brick façade of the house ran parallel with the street, or rather the highway. Behind the door hung an overcoat with a short cape, a bridle, and a black leather cap, and on the ground in the corner stood a pair of riding boots still caked with dried mud . . .

He could see it all. He imagined to himself this house, this vestibule, which probably smelled of leather and horse sweat, then the dining room, where *canary-yellow wallpaper, embellished along the top by a border of pale flowers, was badly hung and all atremble.* He could see it all. Nałęcz, the lakes, Monika, this whole flat, one-dimensional world ceased to exist. He entered Charles Bovary's home, as real as could be, because it was built on the firm, dependable ground of the imagination. No fire, storm, or war could destroy the Bovarys' home, just as the person would never be born who could move the bridle from the vestibule to the alcove or finally rehang the wallpaper in the dining room. Nothing could happen in that closed and yet so hospitable world where every traveler could enter, at any time and of their own free will, without being asked where they came from, what they desired, and what they believed in. And everyone who came here came with their own idea of the smells and sounds, landscapes and emotions of the heart.

The boy suddenly thought that there did not exist only one smell of the black leather cap, just as there was not one bridle hanging by the coat with the short cape. Everyone who found themselves in that cold, dark vestibule . . . He realized in a flash that even the dark and cold were his own property, because someone else, reading that fragment, could have the impression that the vestibule was stuffy and sunlit, and might notice, for example, in the corner an old empty wine barrel or a cat stretching out on the roughly planed floor.

Nothing here was finished, but everything was started. He had to accept the coat, the cap, the bridle, but he could add to it a gander or a wine barrel, a cat or a turkey-cock, shadow or light, cold or heat.

It was a jungle through which everyone had to struggle alone, according to their own inclinations and knowledge and, above all, the liveliness of their imagination. It wasn't possible to change the direction of the journey, and the final destination became known on the last page of the book; yet what significance could that have compared to the vastness of the world that each reader peopled and furnished in their own way, in order to inhabit it, and then, after finishing the book, to take that whole world with them, without altering the smallest fragment of what had been created, so that others could come in turn, live there, and take whole fistfuls of it . . .

He didn't notice that he'd been hooked, but as soon as he had sat on the edge of the bed and opened the book he had hoped he would be. Time passed unnoticed. When he was called to the dining room, he walked down the stairs with Emma Bovary on his arm. They had lunch staring into each other's eyes, unaware of what they were eating. Emma had Monika's face, but despite this she was the wife of Charles Bovary, the kindhearted doctor who was incapable of comprehending the mysteries of her soul.

Over dessert he came to and grew morose. Pudding, father, Miss Cecylia—how obvious all this was! On his way back upstairs he took three steps at a time. For goodness' sake, what had gotten into Charles Bovary's head that he decided to operate on Hippolyte's foot! He was worried about what would happen to Charles, whom he sympathized with. But he was sufficiently well-read to realize that all this would not end well.

At a quarter after seven, when he heard Monika's voice, for a moment he reproached himself for being a traitor. He hadn't noticed that she was back. He slid the book under his pillow and called himself a traitor once again. He went downstairs.

When he looked back he saw Pilecki on the veranda. He was standing with his legs planted wide apart, saying something to the major, who was sitting in a wicker chair.

Monika said:

"Hurry up . . . "

They entered the dense thickets of acacia. It was cold. There was a barking from the kennels behind the barn. But the boy could hear only his own heart.

So she did it after all, he was thinking. She came to meet me halfway. She was able to distract their attention. She pulled the wool over their eyes. Before they knew it we'd disappeared from the veranda. . . . Why couldn't I do that? I'm useless, everything happens outside of me, without my participation. And she's wonderful, the most wonderful person in the world.

They emerged from the bushes onto the path leading toward the lake, Monika in the lead. She was wearing a dress and a shawl thrown loosely over her shoulders. As she walked she tore off alder leaves. He followed behind her.

"What did you do all day?" she asked.

"I read."

"Were you studying?"

"No. It was a novel. *Madame Bovary*."

"What was it about?"

He thought for a moment.

"About a woman and her unhappy husband."

"What about her?" asked Monika.

"She was unhappy too."

Monika shook her head as if with aversion, but she said: "That's the kind of book I like. About unhappy people."

"Why?"

They came out onto the shore of the lake. The water lapped gently against the glistening pebbles.

"Because it's true," said Monika. "People aren't happy in real life either."

She stopped and looked at the boy.

"Do you know that Mrs. Woźnicka is very seriously ill? She's lost weight and has difficulty getting around. She stays in bed for days on end. Today she got up because she's very fond of us."

The boy bent down, picked up a pebble, and threw it into the water. It made a splash. Circles appeared on the surface. Monika said:

"Uncle thinks she'll die soon. It's terrible. What will Mr. Woźnicki do then?"

"Don't think about it," said the boy. He imagined Mrs. Woźnicka lying in a casket, and next to her a stooped man in a dark suit standing and crying. Again he bent down and again threw a pebble into the water. He had the feeling that Monika was slipping away; he sought words that would keep her, but he couldn't find them.

"How awful it all is," said Monika. "You have no idea about it, you live in Warsaw, but here . . ."

"People die in Warsaw too," he said quietly, and remembered Uncle Franciszek's funeral. A military band had played; sunlight glinted off the brass of the trumpets, the hearse moved majestically through the streets, and passersby doffed their caps.

"That's not what I mean," said Monika. "Of course they die. But there everything is different. Here people are poor."

"They are in Warsaw, too," said the boy. Anger was taking hold of him. He felt like shouting, breaking a branch, or hitting something. Anything. Even the trunk of a tree.

"Monika," he murmured, and went up to her. She raised her eyes. She stared at him. She must have been able to hear the pounding of his heart. He felt sweat on his forehead and dryness in his throat. He lifted his hand and put it on the girl's shoulder. She continued to look him in the eye. And he looked at her, but could see only the bright, indistinct blur of her face. He didn't desire her at all now, maybe he didn't even love her; he was permeated with nothing but the will to see things through, at any cost, even at the cost of life—he had to kiss her on the lips, because otherwise he would quite simply cease to exist, just as the day ceases to exist without the sun, a tree without roots, the wind without leaves.

"Monika," he repeated very softly, but he couldn't hear himself and couldn't understand, because he was alone and lacked the strength to know anything beyond the knowledge of that necessity.

His hand tightened on her shoulder; her shawl slowly slipped down. His lips moved closer; now they could feel each other's breath, light, shallow as the breath of someone dying. The boy's other arm rose up, froze for a moment, then dropped heavily on the girl's back. She said something he didn't catch and didn't understand. He felt warmth on his lips, and his head spun from a curious smell of water, leaves, bread, milk, and fruit. He pressed his lips to hers; he saw darkness before him, intersected by blades of light that cut into him. Great millstones turned within him and outside him; stars fell, rivers flowed, slim tree trunks rose skyward, countless armies of fast-moving ants crossed the earth, shadows laid themselves in ragged canyons, shadows laid themselves on mountaintops, the sun shone in the ocean, a horse galloped by, tall grasses thrashed its hindquarters, bees and pitchers, ploughshares covered in moist black earth, he caught a huge fish, he caught a fish as big as a ship, its scales burned with an open fire, where had the world gotten to, people, the good Lord in all His many forms, Baby Jesus among the animals, Christ yellowed on the cross, Madonnas galloped by, angels and devils, he saw animals, he saw people, he saw nothing other than the darkness intersected with blades of light, ice, pressure, pincers, the wing of a dead bird, he saw this and did not see it, he saw *came about*, he saw *happened*, he trembled with an indescribable, apprehensive joy—and then she returned his kiss. He opened his eyes, saw her cheek at an angle, her lowered eyelid, her temple, and a strand of her hair. He felt her mouth, immeasurably delicate; he opened his lips and passed his hand across her slender back. The shawl fell to the ground. Monika pulled back. Perhaps she said something, perhaps not. She picked up the shawl and threw it across her shoulders. She walked off. He followed her. Again she began pulling leaves off the alders.

They both moved slowly, as if in a swamp. Water plashed against the pebbles on the beach. Everywhere there was mist, transparent and bluish. The trees, the lake. The boy touched the girl's arm, drew her to him, and kissed her again. He felt her breasts under her dress; he put his hand on them.

"No," she said.

Again he drew the shawl aside and slid his hand under the material of her dress.

"No," said Monika.

He paid no attention, gripped by a savage greed. Beneath his hand he felt her warm, naked body; he was choking with urgency.

"No," said Monika.

Anger suddenly awoke within him, but it was already too late. Monika was walking ahead of him again, and the water was splashing on the rocks.

I'll marry her, thought the boy. I'll wait a while, then I'll marry her.

Everything passed, and only then did he experience an immense joy.

"Monika," he said gently. "I'll marry you."

She was silent.

"Do you hear me?"

She looked at him intently.

"I'm afraid," she said. "Uncle said there'll be war."

"Oh, he can say what he likes," said the boy, but he had an uneasy feeling. He suddenly thought that if war broke out it would separate him and Monika. That's not possible, he thought.

"There won't be any war," he said. "And even if there is, it'll be over quickly."

But he no longer believed it. He moved close to the girl again, took her in his arms, and they kissed desperately, helplessly, two children, two people, who knew they were doomed.

That night he hardly slept at all. Everything was changing inside him. Shadow was turning into light, light into shadow. He wasn't even thinking a great deal. Rather, he allowed images to pass before his closed eyes, as if he were drowning in the lake—because he had once heard that a drowning person's life flashes before them in every last detail. At one time that made him laugh, because he couldn't understand how the living can know what a drowning person sees. But now he thought solemnly about himself drowning in the lake.

Nothing that had happened in his life was now important or worth remembering. He parted from this accumulation of memories without regret. When it came down to it, he was empty. It was only around himself that he could perceive certain objects, events, and people that had once constituted the entire content of his life. They'll forgive me, he thought, because he felt a little guilty.

As he allowed the images to float by, he was accompanied by Monika. She was with him always and everywhere, and it was only her presence that permitted him to deal forbearingly with the world. When he recalled the pony named Eliza, it was climbing up the steep lane with Monika on its back. And grandmother said: "What a pretty young lady you are, Monika!" And she went on eating cherries from a bag.

Something was poking him under the pillow. He took out the book.

Poor Mrs. Bovary, he thought. She'll forgive me too. . . . And he put the book on the bedside table.

Suddenly he remembered the war. The trenches and the barbed wire. Blood-soaked bandages, wounded soldiers in the field hospital, sisters of mercy. They had tiny porcelain faces and frightened eyes. They were alien. Nonsense, he said to himself, there won't be any war. But he didn't dispel his fear. He wasn't afraid of the trenches, the barbed wire, or even of being wounded. But the thought of losing Monika filled him with despair. I'm fifteen, he repeated bitterly. Why so young? He came to the conclusion that his youth was a curse. If he had at least been three or four years older. . . . He declared to himself that an eighteen-year-old is completely grown up, but he didn't feel convinced. He knew boys who had graduated from high school that year. They were only a little taller than him, and even that not always, not every one. Some of them proudly displayed unshaven chins. Occasionally he met them downtown, strutting along with young ladies. They were stiff, and gave off the scent of brilliantine and birch-water cologne. Some of them wore long pants. Several appeared outside the school immediately after the final exams, wearing student's caps. They behaved imperiously. Then they disappeared, and he never saw them again. But they couldn't convince him they were mature people. He had the impression that he was distinguished from them by a trifle, something intangible but important, which however was easily obtained. Whereas all of them together, they and he, were in a different world, which was set apart from the world of his father, his mother, his grandmother, and also Justyna. Monika was closer to that world than the boys in their caps passing by the schoolhouse, an expression of contempt on their faces. He found it in her eyes. It was as if her eyes lost their luster, dulled by the lake, the green of the woods, the shadow of the barns, the presence of Pilecki and the old ladies, and also the sickness of the woman in Niemirów whose name he had forgotten.

If war breaks out, he thought, I'll lose her forever.

And he was seized by despair.

Breakfast didn't last long. The shadows of leaves danced on the veranda, and people, caught in this net, moved sluggishly. Pilecki stared at the boy. In his eyes there was something sickly, sorrow and anger. The boy's parents exchanged glances across the table and ate in silence. Miss Cecylia took tiny sips of tea watered down with milk. Miss Róża wasn't there; she had stayed in bed because of a cold.

Monika was absent too. The boy suddenly felt threatened. He wanted to ask what had happened to Monika, but he lacked the courage. He looked toward the door that led to the rest of the house, in the hope that the girl would appear soon. Minutes went by. She didn't come.

Mania came in with a tray. She looked at the boy. In pain and in sympathy, it seemed to him.

All at once Major Kurtz announced that he had to return to Warsaw.

"I've just had an urgent telegram summoning me," he said.

"So that's how things stand after all," put in the boy's father.

"It doesn't necessarily mean anything," replied the major. "Just routine army business."

"I admire you," said Pilecki tartly. "We all have within us inexhaustible reserves of hopes and illusions."

As he spoke, he gazed at the boy. The boy looked to the side.

"I assure you, ladies and gentlemen," said Kurtz, "that in two days I'll be back."

"I think she'll die after all," said Miss Cecylia out of the blue.

Everyone looked at the old lady. Her watery eyes expressed embarrassment. She smiled apologetically.

"I keep thinking about the attorney's wife," she said quietly.

"Yes," Pilecki took up. "Mrs. Woźnicka is in a bad way."

"If war were to break out . . ." said Miss Cecylia.

"Not everyone dies in wartime," put in Major Kurtz help-fully. "Besides, there's no question of that, ma'am. As I said, in a few days I'll be back and the captain and I will go duck-hunting again."

The boy was listening and was somewhere else. Monika, what's happening? Where are you? he was thinking. She got up early today and went for a walk, he answered himself, but he immediately recalled the illusions Pilecki had spoken of. Why was he addressing himself to me? Why was he looking at me like that?

The fear in him grew.

Mania reappeared, bringing cold milk in a jug. And again she looked at the boy with a sorrowful eye, the way wise old animals look.

All of a sudden he had a revelation, and calmed down. Mania was sad because the major was leaving with his little soldier. What a relief!

He drank a full glass of milk. He relaxed. Poor, dear Mania. Don't worry, he said to her wordlessly. In two days they'll both be back. You alone ought to know that we're not in danger of war. Mania, you have no idea how much I like you . . .

He followed her out with a more cheerful look. He reached for a second glass of milk, took a sip, and had the impression he was kissing Monika. There won't be any war; everything will turn out well.

Pilecki stood up from the table. He was sorry, but he had to drive to the village on business. The chaise for the good major was ready to depart.

The major stood too; they embraced warmly, and Pilecki said:

"I'd like to believe in that hunting trip!"

He went off toward the barns. Kurtz sat down. He lit a cigarette, and the boy's father, a cigar.

Then his mother turned to the boy and said:

"After breakfast come upstairs."

"All right," he replied. "Straight away?"

"I think so," put in his father.

Miss Cecylia looked at the boy and said:

"What lovely weather. I bet Krzyś is thinking about going for a swim in the lake."

Suddenly he felt her hand on his own. It was cold and frail. The smooth fingertips moved up to his wrist.

"Krzyś is a very good boy. Actually, he's almost grown up."

"Not quite," said the boy's father.

"My dear," said Miss Cecylia gently and withdrew her hand. "What do we know about those close to us? I'm a very old woman."

The boy's father gave a sour smile.

"Let's not be afraid," said the old lady. "It's not much, and yet it's a lot."

The boy felt fear once again. Something bad was happening with the world.

He stood in the small room. Behind him was the window, and outside the window the sun. There was a smell of powder. His mother's small face looked haggard. Her head was bowed, and the file she was using to shape her nails flashed coldly. His father was slowly lighting a cigar.

"What do you think you're up to?" he asked harshly, staring at the flame of the match.

The boy said nothing. In his mouth he had the taste of honey and milk. A moment ago they had finished breakfast on the veranda.

"Well?" said his father.

The boy shrugged. He raised his hand to his forehead and combed his fingers through his hair.

"Leave your hair alone," said his mother. "It's about time you understood certain things."

"Yes, Mama," he said and dropped his hand. He rested it on the windowsill behind him. The sunlight warmed his back. Where's Monika? he was thinking. What has happened?

"What's happened?" he asked.

"You know perfectly well what's happened," said his father. He was supposedly looking the boy in the eye, but he blew out cigar smoke so as to separate himself from the rest of the world with an ash-gray screen.

"We're guests here," said his mother, setting aside her nail file. "That carries certain obligations. One has to behave decently. I had hoped that you were properly brought up. What's going on with you, Krzysztof?"

Again she was calling him by his name, which indicated a reprimand, a letdown, and also the defenselessness of this woman.

"I don't understand," replied the boy.

His father walked across the room, but there wasn't much space and he had to do something with that big, heavy body of his, so he sat down on a chair.

"Captain Pilecki is an old friend of mine," said his father. "I respect him. You must respect him too. Understood?"

"What's happened?" repeated the boy, though by now he knew everything.

"Monika is a well-bred young lady," said his mother. "Am I making myself clear? You're acting like a little scoundrel. It's a disgrace!"

She raised her voice, but didn't lift her head. She went on sitting bent over on the side of the bed, as if she felt uncomfortable in her role as admonishing moralizer. And it was indeed not the part for her.

"Why a scoundrel?" asked the boy. "Because we went for a walk down by the lake?"

"Don't act dumb!" said his father. "Walk, my foot . . . You're a kid, Krzysztof. You're only fifteen. What were you thinking of? Captain Pilecki is really indignant. And hurt!"

Suddenly the boy felt angry. A warm, stormy current passed through him. He pulled his hands from the windowsill and passed all ten fingers through his hair.

"I'm fifteen," he said dully. "What of it? It's not my fault I'm fifteen."

He wanted to add something else, but he lost his train of thought. Once again, as yesterday on the shore of the lake, he heard the rumbling hubbub of the world. He was oppressed by the fact that he had to stand, with the sun hot on his back. He wanted to lie down, relax all of his muscles; he felt unutterably tired, and ached as if he had been mercilessly beaten.

"Miss Monika is leaving for Niemirów today," said the boy's mother. "She doesn't wish to see you. How could you do something like this to us?"

Darkness. The whole room became dim, darkness was everywhere. It pulsed through the boy along with his blood. He gave a grating sigh. He wanted to say something but couldn't express it; he couldn't find the right words, the word *Monika*, the word *war*, the words *I'll die*, the word *love*, some other word too, grotesque, unknown, perhaps nonexistent, which was despair, blasphemy, a bitter, thick spittle that filled his mouth. He thought: I hate you all. He thought: I love you, Monika. He thought: I'm dying. He thought: God! He thought: War will come, it'll come tomorrow, it'll kill off all of them, without mercy, in torment, me too . . .

His father spoke quietly to his mother:

"What's wrong with him? I asked you not to say anything!"

"Oh, come off it," retorted his mother. "It'll pass."

She stood up, smoothed her skirt, and went up to the boy.

"Aren't you feeling well, sweetheart?"

He saw her and did not see her.

He said:

"Go away, Mama."

She turned pale; her features sharpened, and she said, almost in a whisper:

"My Lord, this is awful."

Now the boy's father came up. He moved his mother aside, gently and roughly at the same time.

He said with an effort, looking the boy in the eyes:

"What's wrong with you? Maybe there's been a mistake."

"Go away," said the boy, but he couldn't hear his own voice. The world was still roaring.

"Maybe there's been a mistake," repeated his father and at once added calmly, in a measured tone: "Of course, a mistake."

He returned to his chair. He sat down. A weak, old man.

Silence fell. The boy's mother leaned against the wardrobe. The boy crossed the room, opened the door, went out, closed the door.

Then he heard his father's voice saying:

"Something has come to an end, darling."

He went down the stairs, then along the hallway to the playroom and the veranda. The sun was unbearably hot. Squat, oval-shaped shadows on the lawn. The clatter of horses' hooves. The boy raised his eyes. A horse was galloping down the avenue. A glob of foam splashed onto the acacia bushes. Pilecki was standing in the stirrups, leaning over the horse's mane. They passed by the lawn; clods of earth spattered wetly against one of the columns of the veranda, and a trail of sweat and hot leather followed in their wake.

He'll be the first to die, thought the boy vengefully. Those German tanks will blow out his guts.

He went down the avenue toward the gate. He could see hoofprints in the earth. Then he followed the road in the direction of the village. And for a long time he could see nothing, because he was crying.

Now, when his tears dried, he would return to the manor. He would walk into Monika's room, and she would take him in her arms. Before the eyes of everyone they would walk out of there together, leaving his mother and father, her uncle and the old ladies, the dolls, teddy bears, Indian bows, sailing boats made of tree bark and rings bought at church fairs, that whole paradise of childhood which God had once taken away from Adam and Eve. They would go away, united and joyful, and after a long and arduous journey they would cross the bridge over the Vistula in Warsaw and begin a new life. He would work in the sweat of his brow, and she would cover his damp forehead with loving kisses. And they would live happily ever after.

Now, when his tears dried, he would return to the manor. He would walk into Monika's room, but he would find only lifeless furniture and the dust of abandoned hopes. He would be alone as never before and as never again in the future that still awaited him. Then he would meet another girl. The day would come when he could no longer summon from memory Monika's face, her voice, her gestures, or the color of her dress. He would suffer a little, but his thoughts would soon return to his machines, lancets, or court records. And it would be another day, perhaps at dusk, or perhaps just before sunrise, that he would look about and see an empty platform, and at the end of it a dark tunnel toward which he was ineluctably moving; then Monika would stand before him, and once again he would feel her lips and hear the plash of the waters of the lake washing against the pebbles on the shore.

Now, when his tears dried, he would walk forward alone. On the horizon something was already flashing; the earth was swelling, the blaze was spreading all around. He would walk forward, toward the war, which was coming toward him. They would meet. His mouth sealed with plaster, he would find himself on the execution ground. He would be buried under the rubble of a collapsed building. The airtight door of the gas chamber would close behind him. He would die of his wounds. He would survive. He would be a young, old man. He would visit Nałęcz. He would kneel among the graves and say a prayer for the people there. As he was leaving he would meet an old lady at the cemetery gate, and it would be Miss Cecylia.

Now, when his tears dried, he would no longer be a child.